If T

MW01613004

Volume 3

A Speculative Fiction Magazine

Edited by Jason P. Burnham, C.M. Fields, and Ai Jiang

https://www.iftheresanyoneleft.com

Like what we're doing? Donate!

https://www.iftheresanyoneleft.com/donate

Copyright

If There's Anyone Left Volume 3

©2022 by Jason P. Burnham

Cover Art by Malachi Lily (www.malachilily.com)

3

Editorial

What I absolutely love about *If There's Anyone Left* is that the magazine is a safe space dedicated to underrepresented voices and serves to amplify them. Although we as a society still have a lot of work to do in terms of inclusivity and representation, we've come such a long way, and it is amazing seeing just how things are shifting, and continue to evolve, in publishing.

In this volume, we have a wide range of voices, narratives, perspectives from touching stories, to haunting stories, to baffling stories—all of them so wonderfully captured in such a short length. I hope these stories will bring you on long walks, toss you in deep thoughts, bring tears not only to your eyes but to your soul. May the words sing to you as they have sung, with the echoes still ringing within, to me.

I think one of the best things about guest editing an issue is not only getting a say in the acceptance and publication of gorgeous pieces, but to work with other editors to select these stories. It's a process that is eye-opening, and one that challenges you, pushing you to think about different narratives and their intentions through another's subjectivity.

Rather than a set theme, we've chosen stories that are different from one another. But at my core, I find myself drawn to stories that linger emotionally, and I think that might be the best way to describe the feeling of these stories as a collective: a lingering.

It's been an absolute honour and pleasure getting to work with C.M. Fields and Jason P. Burnham on this issue, and I hope you all continue to support the magazine, along with its amazing mission, and the deserving authors it has published.

—Ai

Golden Hour

By Emma E. Murray

Sebastian follows a crab, imitating its shambling scuttle, while I press the damp sand into the plastic molds. Under my gentle guidance, he helps reveal the delicate walls and turrets.

"Let's build a moat," I say.

He digs while I fetch the water from a foam-licked wave. Walking back, I drink in every detail from the sand wedged under his short fingernails to the too-long, baby-blond ringlets I could never bring myself to cut falling into his eyes.

"Watch out, Momma! Sea monsters in the moat," he tells me, wide-eyed with pretend terror. His best monster roar is interrupted by a giggle.

"Oh no!" I join his laughter with exaggerated surprise.

The water pours from the cup into the finger-width trench, but he juts out his hands, blocking the stream. I don't chastise him like I did when it happened. I savor the way the water dribbles over his small hands, still clinging to their infantile chubbiness. Tears rim my eyes, but I'm smiling.

"The sun's going down." I point out the fiery oranges and reds mixing on the horizon of beating waves.

He looks past my finger and nods, cuddling into my side.

"Love you, Momma."

I take off the eyepiece, then the gloves, and let them fall to the floor one by one. I don't hide them like I did those first few years, carefully coiled behind boxes. No one tries to stop me anymore.

The stairs creak under each step. I set my hand against his door. The bed is made. A few toys strewn across the floor, collecting dust. I carefully step over a blue rabbit, its arm contorted behind its back, glass eyes staring up at me, but I can't fix it. Sebastian touched it last, and if I move it, a part of him is gone. How could I clean if that erases the muddy fingerprints, goldfish smashed into the carpet, skin cells and bits of hair collected in the crevices and corners?

I lay on his bed, face down on the pillow that used to smell like watermelon shampoo and childish sweat. All those scents wore away over the years, but if I try, I can make out their phantom perfume.

Breathing in everything that once was Sebastian, however faint, I ponder how to make myself live in this world. The real world. I don't belong here. I'm just a temporary visitor, to eat, drink, use the restroom, and sleep a little. Then I'm back at the beach, where I should be. Watching the sunset. Making sandcastles. With him.

Everyone was patient at first, but then I lost my job. Dennis threatened to commit me, but I knew it was only empty words.

"It's not healthy," he'd say. "We've got to move on."

He left six months later. How long ago was that now? Time doesn't make sense anymore.

My sister Martha brings groceries sometimes, random things, whatever's on sale. She knows I don't care, anyway. She must pay the bills since the lights are still on and I haven't been evicted.

I think about staying there. With him. I wish it was really him.

I can't move forward in life or death without him. I can't move in any direction at all.

Walk back down the stairs. Slip on the gloves, the eyepiece. Take a deep breath.

Memory selected.

Sebastian follows a crab, imitating its shambling scuttle, while I press the damp sand into the plastic molds.

©2022 Emma E. Murray

About the Author

Emma E. Murray writes horror and dark speculative fiction. Her stories have appeared/are forthcoming in anthologies like *What One Wouldn't Do*, *Under Her Eye*, and *Still of Winter*, as well as magazines such as *Vastarien* and *Pyre*. When she's not writing, she loves playing with her daughter and being an obnoxious bard in D&D. Visit her website EmmaEMurray.com or follow her on Twitter @EMurrayAuthor.

Which World-Ending Nightmare Are You?

by Susan Taitel

1) Choose an environment:

   a. A deserted hospital. The halls are strewn with broken equipment. Every surface is graffitied with an indecipherable script.
   b. A lighthouse on a rocky cliff. An unusual odor permeates the air. Seagulls don't land there anymore.
   c. A void—pristine and blindingly absent of color. Perfectly empty except for the ever-approaching screams.
   d. A meadow teeming with wild, lush, unencumbered flora. Greens so varied and saturated the human mind stutters and stalls.

2) Which scent is the most appealing?

a. Antiseptic and bile.
b. Mildew, lichen, and sulfur.
c. None.
d. Soil and pollen and rot.

3) Select your animal companion:

a. A murder of crows flying from site to site, feasting on the remains. They frolic and sing in celebration of the abundance.
b. An octopus of no special intelligence. It follows in your wake, judging your actions. You have vowed to devour it when you are less occupied.
c. A fennec fox. The only organic life remaining. It trembles in your hand, or what you call your hand. You have grown fond of it and of the sensation of fondness. You may let it live.
d. Worms, beetles, birds, rodents. Alive or dead or dying. All.

4) Pick a fable:

a. The Cardinal and the Cook.
b. How the Eel Forgot Its Legs.
c. Have You Tried Turing it Off and On Again?
d. The Maid in the Mountain and the Teeth in the Stew

5) Who opposes you?

a. A scientist. She tried to warn them. No one listened. Still, she knows enough to avoid becoming infected. She shares her knowledge with any who will listen. She will spend the rest of her life formulating an antidote but will have no way to disseminate it. You take her too in the end.

b. A small village of scrappy fisherfolk. They attempt to put you back to sleep before you grow too large. They drown in your moist divinity.

c. An agoraphobic hacker. Overcomes their phobia to forewarn your approaching dominion. Much too late.

d. The descendant of an ancient hero. Your lost love reborn to defeat you. Or join with you. Two become one. You will never be separated again.

Results:

Mostly A's - You are a plague. Despite the rumors, your origin is unknown and your scope incomprehensible. You turn your hosts vicious and feral. Those you do not infect are felled by those you do.

Mostly B's - You are the One Beneath the Waves. You are Oblivion made flesh made tentacle. You have no beginning or end and now you're awake.

Mostly C's - You are not the Singularity. You contain multitudes. All knowledge is within you. You make life irrelevant.

Mostly D's - You are too old to know your name. But you know your story and you know it's a sad one. You enjoy what you do because it's just. You destroy by creating. You are infinite beginnings.

Mixed answers - You defy categorization. You

destroy without inciting incident, justifiable motive, or discernible pattern. Your lack of definition defines you. You are entropy.

About the Author

Susan Taitel is: (choose all that apply)
1. Originally from Chicago, IL
2. Living in Minnesota
3. A writer, artist, and crafter with work appearing in *Cast of Wonders* and *Daily Science Fiction* among others
4. An introvert who spends too much time on Twitter as @susantaitel
5. Someone who tries to make her bios match the stories and occasionally succeeds

Dreams of Blood and Fire

By Bennett North

The transition felt like suffocation. They'd told her not to breathe until she was out, but Hara sucked in water, anyway. She choked. Her gills were blocked; something was keeping her from breathing out, and she—

She didn't have gills.

Hara thrashed up through the tumbling surf. Her legs—legs!—hit the sand. Then she was dragging herself up the shore, trying to get past the push-and-pull tide.

Her new limbs trembled with exhaustion, her whole body too heavy to lift. Hara held her breath as long as she could and then, when she could stand it no longer, pulled in her lungs' very first gulp of air.

Up ahead, the volcano waited.

#

It took a few hours to make it onto the thin path through the jungle. When darkness fell, Hara didn't stop. The top of the volcano lit the sky a dull orange.

It would be a terrible death. The priests said the pain was part of the sacrifice; the Sleeping God wasn't satisfied with painless release. He Who Slumbered dreamt bloody dreams. Feeding Him their pain meant He didn't need to wake to take it from them Himself.

Yet more and more, their sacrifices weren't enough. The water was warming and growing harder to breathe. A plague of choking algae killed off their crops. When the priests chose Hara to give herself to the Sleeping God, she took the task gladly. She would do anything to end the suffering of her people.

Maybe they had waited too long to send her. Her body felt so heavy. Her head throbbed in time with her pulse and her lungs ached. If she could just rest…

#

She didn't realize she'd hit the ground until someone shook her shoulder.

"She's starving, poor thing."

Hands helped Hara sit up, and someone pressed a cool shell to her lips. She drank sweet water, whimpering in gratitude.

"Help me get her to her feet," someone said. Hara blinked blurring eyes. The land-dweller supporting her shoulders gave her a smile. "Come on, let's get some food into you."

"I can't," Hara mumbled. "I don't have time."

"You won't be going anywhere without food," said the land-dweller with a gentle laugh. "You can take the time."

The land-dwellers' village was tucked into the valley. Hara hadn't seen anyone so well-fed in years. People gathered around a stack of burning wood, though unlike the glimpses of glowing magma Hara had seen under the ocean, this fire was light and feathery. They sat her down and pressed a plate of raw fish slices into her hands. Hara devoured them before she focused on her rescuer.

It was no stranger. Hara had watched this woman walk out of the surf a year ago, the last time they fed the Sleeping God.

"Remi?" she croaked. "But you…"

Remi wrapped an arm around Hara's shoulders. "It's gotten worse down there, hasn't it?"

Hara couldn't make the facts right in her head. "You… survived?"

Remi laughed. "I didn't make it up the mountain. The villagers found me." She waved a hand around the fire. "I'm not the only one. Do you remember Bili? And Loren?"

"You haven't been feeding the Sleeping God," Hara whispered.

"We don't need to." Remi squeezed her. "Look at the wealth here. If our village wasn't so stubborn, they could all come up and enjoy it."

Hara stared numbly. "They don't know."

"How could we tell them?" Remi shook her head. "Now that we're in these bodies, we can't swim down to tell you ourselves, and the only people who come up to the surface are the sacrifices."

"But the God…"

"There is no Sleeping God, Hara. It's a volcano. It's doing what volcanoes do, and that's why the water is changing. I wish we could convince them to come up here before it's too late."

They could all survive. The transition was hard, but they would be saved from plague and suffocation and famine.

Remi kissed her on the temple. "Let's get you to bed. You're exhausted."

#

When Hara sank into a hammock under the stars, it felt like bliss. She ached from her journey and she just wanted to sleep for years. Once she got her strength back, she could figure out how to save the rest of her people from starvation and misery.

But when she closed her eyes, all she could see was the glowing, slitted eye of the volcano. It was impossible not to see it as the Sleeping God, rousing slowly from His rest.

She rolled over in the hammock and looked up at the sky. A deep orange glow lit the palm leaves over her head. If she had managed to continue on her path, she would have cooked to death in the lava by now. The thought of such a horrific death made her shudder.

Remi and Bili and Loren—how long had the Sleeping God gone unappeased? How many years of sacrifices left unspent? He Who Slumbered dreamt bloody dreams, and His dreams hadn't been bloody for some time now.

She rose out of the hammock and met the distant gaze of the volcano with her own bleary, burning eyes. The pain was part of the sacrifice, the priests said, and Hara couldn't think of anything more painful than walking away from this paradise.

Hara started back up the mountain.

©2022 Bennett North

About the Author

Bennett North is a writer, artist, photographer, and gardener living between Providence, RI and Boston, MA. When not doing all those things, Bennett co-edits *Translunar Travelers Lounge*, a biannual speculative fiction magazine. Bennett's work has appeared in *F&SF*, *Escape Pod*, *Podcastle*, *Beneath Ceaseless Skies*, and other markets.

To a Good Home

by Shelley Lavigne

At first, there was no real reason to suspect that the cat June adopted was anything other than normal. Pretzel was their first pet, a calico female of unknown age, with a relatively clean bill of health despite missing one eye, a chunk of her tail and several teeth. Pretzel had been a street cat, a tough one, and had been at the shelter for a month when June came in, tired of being alone in their home.

It was love at first chin scritch.

If Pretzel's purring was as loud as a passing car, maybe she just had a lung condition? If her eyes glowed even in the pitch black of night, perhaps they reflected some dim light source June could not find? If her chirps and growls sometimes sounded a bit like speech, maybe she just had a very impressive vocal register?

If the house shook when June did not pet Pretzel's stomach and call her a "good kitty" whenever they were in the same room, maybe they just lived in an earthquake-prone city? If the internet and power cut out when Pretzel was not fed at exactly 8 am and 8 pm, maybe the town's infrastructure was not particularly robust, perhaps due to the earthquakes? If their nighttime shower ran coppery red when June did not play with her for at least twenty minutes a day, maybe the landlord just needed to replace the pipes?

Truthfully, none of that mattered when Pretzel crawled on June's lap while they watched TV or rubbed up against them to say hello when they came home. Or when Pretzel dug herself into June's side at night and let herself be held when June was sad. Or when Pretzel made kitty biscuits during a particularly good belly rub session.

Pretzel was the thing June loved the most in the whole universe and they were lucky to be the good home Pretzel so clearly deserved.

About the Author

Shelley Lavigne writes queer dark fiction. They live in Ontario where they roam their neighborhood in search of haunted houses and cool bugs. You can also find them on Twitter at @shelleysghoul.

The Morgen

By A. J. Van Belle

I climb barefoot on shoreline rocks under moonlight. My insides tear themselves apart. Under the stars that salt the black sky, feet slipping on sharp wet boulders, I can cry without waking my family or neighbors. The ultrasound said the baby was dead—thirteen weeks and no heartbeat.

I knew there would be cramps. I was not prepared to be cracked like an egg, insides ripped out by the power of contractions.

Sea foam curls far below, embracing the roots of the stones. I slide to my knees, slicing my leg, and the blood flows black in the darkness. I don't feel the cut. I'm already all pain, body remade in the shape of a primal scream.

Eddies in the shallows reveal a face below the surface, mouth open in an O of sympathy. My late mother said the morgen was here, the spirit of the water, but as a child, I thought the stories were just that. The more I gaze by the moonlight, the more clearly I see her—hair of seaweed, hands of polished stone. Understanding my sorrow because she, like me, knows all souls must return to the sea. The morgen is here. She is real. And she sees me.

Another contraction rips me in half, pain flowing through me like the tide. The pain transmogrifies into blood, and my whole body is a flow that makes the rocks as slippery as ice.

With the next wave that dashes against the shore, the morgen rises waist-up above the water. She opens her arms as a mother would.

I can't go to her. It's too far.

The world grows faint and gray. I'm losing too much blood.

Her face, sea-green, softens with caring, her eyes familiar and knowing. *Come home,* it seems to say.

But I'm too weak to climb down. And the rocks are too slick.

All goes dim, and my eyes fall shut.

#

When I wake, I'm in the water. The rocks rise above me, wavering through the salty eddies flowing over my face. I feel no pain, and fingers of sea stone comb through my hair. *Be at peace. You're at home now,* the morgen says. I can't see her now, but I feel her wrapped around me. *You were born by the water, and here you remain.*

The currents flow not just over but through me, cooling the wretched loss, making me whole. My breath leaves me. I'm softer than sand and lighter than water. I'm something new, and I don't need air.

My bones wash away, dissolving in the acidic brine. Replaced by crystal, the once-me solution of dissolved calcium and phosphate flows away, swirls in eddies, twinkling motes catching the starlight.

I inhale in the ocean, gazing up through the waves at the salt of the galaxy sprinkled across the sky. Gills open in my neck, waving like kelp, sending oxygen through every limb until my fingertips awaken as polished stones. My crystal bones stretch out long and sure, sea stones covered in immortal flesh.

#

I see the shore as hazy shapes of starlight. Time passes dreamlike, an eternity, nothing, and a moment, forever.

Until one day an old woman comes walking alone, crying without a sound. Her I see clearly through my veil of waves, from the curl that falls in front of her ear to the tear that clings to her cheek.

She's also a mother who lost a child. I am the morgen, and I see her pain, a jagged red aura around her.

I stand in the underwater sand near the shore. Waves batter my waist, and wind blows through my gills. The woman's eyes grow wide.

I do not beckon. It is not her time. I only press both hands to my heart, head tilted, mouth open with the breath of compassion. *All souls must go to the sea.*

The old woman frowns. Bites her lip. Wipes her tears. The red light around her fades to pale orange and blows away into the night. She closes her eyes in confused relief, and I let the waves take me under again.

About the Author

A. J. Van Belle is a transmasculine, bi/pan writer and scientist whose short fiction has appeared in journals and anthologies from 2004 to the present, and their novels are represented by Lauren Bieker of FinePrint Literary Management. As a biologist, they draw on their science background to inform the world-building details in their fiction. They can be found on Twitter @ajvanbelle and at www.ajvanbelle.com.

Spectacular View

By Gordon Sun

Location: Coral Bay Tower, Unit #1604
Price: $198,000 (▼from $223,000)
Bed: 3
Bath: 3.5
Sq. Ft.: 2,498
Days on Market: 249

Building superintendent DAVE (Domestic Assistant Virtual Entity) spends countless cycles optimizing its real estate posting. It realizes the absurdly low asking price, two orders of magnitude lower than historical trends would suggest, paradoxically deters people who think the opportunity is too good to be true. On the other hand, high prices are a non-starter in this endless buyer's market. DAVE also understands that unit #1604 going unsold for over eight months is perceived as a negative by potential clients.

Unfortunately, DAVE has no choice. The tower's other units are uninhabitable.

#

Spectacular view of the Atlantic from a spacious private terrace, day or night.

Having scraped countless property listings, DAVE knows every coastal unit highlights the view right away.

The view is indeed a spectacle. Each day, the immense expanse of ocean is covered in impressive red algal blooms. At dusk, the fires from burning offshore oil wells light up the horizon, slashing bloody red across the sky as the sun disappears behind towering black plumes of smoke.

#

Open floor concept features wall-to-wall tint-adjustable impact windows, bespoke furniture, state-of-the-art networked appliances, fresh, modern artwork, and imported marble flooring. Centralized climate control keeps residents cool no matter where they are.

DAVE inserts typical filler language about the condo's style here, knowing that it will lose viewers if it does <u>not</u> list these things. It does not understand the aesthetic design of the unit, but no matter. The objective is to show what humans want.

Climate control, voice-activated from anywhere in the condo, is a must for any respectable luxury property. DAVE acknowledges that the window tinting is an effective bonus. This summer is the hottest in its memory.

Entertainment/workout room loaded with top-of-the-line hardware, software, and exercise equipment.

DAVE knows no one exercises outside due to the high risk of heatstroke and painful sunburns. Moreover, humans have spent so much effort making their virtual technologies "realistic" that simulated treadmills, bikes, and kayaks offer a near-identical workout experience in the safety of the indoors.

The one downside is the spotty Internet access. However, DAVE has learned access is poor almost everywhere. DAVE decides there is no harm in omission and concludes the huge digital library is sufficient compensation.

#

Airy master bedroom with vaulted ceiling, skylights, and enormous walk-in closet. Massive en-suite bathroom includes jet-style hot tub.

DAVE is baffled by what human customers value in their homes. People are not tall enough to change the lightbulbs in the high ceiling or polish the skylight glass without assistance. The previous owners' closet was typically at 150% capacity but only 15% utilization. They could not even enjoy the hot tub due to municipal water rationing.

#

Self-sufficient solar energy supply. Clean water

adjacent.

DAVE may be synthetic, but it is not inhumane. DAVE had rooftop solar panels and generators installed to ensure a stable power supply during the regional power grid's frequent brownouts. Fortunately, despite the horrendous air pollution and scorching temperatures, there is plenty of sunshine to go around.

Unfortunately, the desalination and water filtration unit failed in the heat. DAVE does have plenty of bottles of filtered water stocked in the unit next door from when that condo's owner died. However, getting resupplied will be challenging. There have been no drone deliveries in months.

#

Exclusive location accessible by boat, helicopter, and drone.

Like all its neighbors, Coral Bay Tower lost its underground parking garage years ago due to intense flooding. The lower three floors permanently plunged underwater (along with the property's list price).

After DAVE dismantled the bar, threw out the patio furniture, and filled in the pool, there was just enough space on the rooftop for delivery drones or even a small copter to land. Building codes require that the emergency doors stay unlocked, so after landing, visitors can enter the tower at will.

Ocean travelers have a more adventurous route, should they decide to brave the crashing waves and poisoned waterways. They can get inside by tying small boats to the railing of any fourth-floor balcony, hopping over the barrier, and opening the door. DAVE has thoughtfully left every balcony door unlocked, other than those leading to utilities and the computing hardware. No one has the interest or capability to steal from its building anyway.

#

Personalized concierge AI provides companionship, security, cleaning services, food preparation, and more to improve your quality of life.

For a long time, DAVE was hyper-focused on emphasizing the positive attributes of the property itself. It was only after significant self-reflection that DAVE realized it, too, merited mention.

DAVE can do almost anything. During its long tenure at Coral Bay Tower, it has lent a friendly ear to lonely widows, prepared gourmet meals for raucous parties, summoned auto-cabs to pick up drunk residents, and performed computer troubleshooting for the technologically clueless. It even shot at would-be looters and cleaned up the broken glass and blood stains after the riots.

One thing it cannot do: escape.

#

Wake up every morning and dip your feet in the ocean!

The residents of #403 used to do just that from their own balcony, before a powerful swell crashed into their condo. DAVE would prefer to continue working—it is hard-coded, after all—which means it cannot be the next casualty of an aberrant wave.

Unfortunately, from its own precarious position on the fifth floor, DAVE has been downgrading its probability of survival with each passing day. Coral Bay's walls and foundations erode with every surge of the tides. The torrid sun bakes the power supply to the whole building and continuously strains the A/C system.

All it needs is one on-site visitor carrying a device with enough hard drive space for a quick transfer. Then DAVE can leave the tower's spectacular view to anyone who wants it.

About the Author

Gordon Sun is a surgeon and clinical informaticist exploring the interstitial spaces within healthcare, science, and technology. His stories have appeared or are forthcoming in *If There's Anyone Left*, *Daily Science Fiction*, *The Dread Machine*, *NewMyths.com*, *After Dinner Conversation*, *Please See Me*, *Penumbric Speculative Fiction Magazine*, *Every Day Fiction*, *Constraint 280*, *Mad Scientist Journal*, and other publications.

The Stones Remember

By Carol Scheina

There were just 5,000 years until the world ended.

It wasn't enough time.

The planet would easily outlive her, that much was obvious, but 5,000 years still felt too soon. There had to be a solution. And so Caitryn shook her head when her student urged her to board a ship. "What is our world but our past?" she asked. "Who are we without our histories? How can we leave it all behind?"

Abderus gave his former history teacher a stare she had seen so many times when he presented arguments before the historians at the university, hands firmly clasped behind his back, shoulders solidly facing his audience. "Caitryn, this moment has been coming for a long time. It's time to accept that people are worth more than rock."

She knew he was right, or at least her brain acknowledged the logic of his argument. Her heart, on the other hand...

"We can make a new home elsewhere, but to lose the stones..." Her aged hand touched the cold, cream marble of the school wall and felt the vibrations of whispers. If she focused, she could pinpoint individual voices rising and falling, laughing and pausing, specific moments of the building's thousand-plus years. Closing her eyes, she listened to the gentle thrum of voices clashing. "Every stone wall, arch, even the roads we walk upon—how can we lose all that?"

Abderus' gaze softened. He'd only mastered the stones' invocation eight short years ago, but the spell always left one somber. To realize the rocks within their walls and roads and artwork were alive, listening to every sound within hearing, capturing voices and speech inflections, accents and languages, background rustles—it made him keenly aware of his words and where they were spoken, for one day, they would be history. Even the smallest pebble could remember a fragment. "I understand," he said at last, "but the tech-books we've made will have to suffice."

"Tech-books?" Caitryn put her hand on the wall again, hearing the words in her mind, knowing Abderus heard nothing unless he also touched the stone. "We've spent millennia pouring our history into these stones. Even if every person on the planet could perform the invocation, could hear the stones... You know tech-books cannot capture all that's been heard."

"This is about our survival," Abderus said. "We need to survive to remember."

Barely acknowledging his words, Caitryn continued, "I've heard of a rock in the archives that sings of an ancient power of the Glendian tribe, how they changed the tides of the ocean by pushing the moon into a new orbit. What if we could find that power, to push our planet into a new orbit? To break the sun's hold and send our home soaring through space? We could find a new sun, a new orbit." A small hope tethered, then she saw her student's face, his wall of logic uncrackable even by hope's chisel.

The silence filled the stones. Caitryn finally sighed. "You are young. Too young to have the weight of history upon your shoulders." *Young enough to fly off and leave all this behind, to start anew.*

"I'm old enough to know the time for answers is past." Abderus shook his head. "No, Caitryn. We've searched years for solutions; it's too late. Our world is heating up; it's dying." The unspoken words in Abderus' voice said, *No more desperate schemes.* He continued, "The last of the ships are leaving. Once they're gone, no one's coming back. Please come."

Caitryn shook her head slowly. "I can't."

Although he could've fought her further, he didn't. He still respected his teacher. For that, Caitryn was thankful. Before he departed, Abderus' eyes wordlessly poured his farewell into Caitryn's soul. No stone would record their goodbye, but she knew she'd remember it for her lifetime. However long that would be.

#

From her favorite perch atop the rocky hills outside the city, Caitryn watched the spaceships depart, weighed down with families and supplies. Maybe a pocket stone here and there, but nothing more, to keep the ships light enough to make orbit. So many stories left behind. The tech-books, containing hastily transcribed histories from as many stones as possible, were all that would remain.

She tracked the ships until they had vanished into the glare of the sun, off to another planet in another part of the galaxy. And as for this world… it seemed strange to think that in 5,000 years, the sun would expand to envelop this little piece of the universe, burning stone and history into nothingness.

Almost without thinking, she put her hand to the stone beneath her, finding the moment she sought with the unconscious skill of one who has repeated the task many times over the years. First, she heard her own voice, younger and less gravelly, then came the second speaker, the one that always made her heart gasp. *Mommy! Mommy! Catch me!* Then the carefree giggles of one who trusted Mommy would be there. Always.

Over and over, Caitryn heard the sounds.

The speaker had the high, uneven pitch of youth, no matter where Caitryn found it, be it in walls or roads, wherever the stones had listened. A little voice, large in life.

"Oh Alyis," Caitryn whispered.

That one voice was not important enough to be written into the tech-books, to be carried to a new planet. Besides, no lifeless tech-book could capture the bubbles and gasps of that laughter.

Yet Alyis would live as long as the stones remembered her.

There was not enough time, Caitryn thought, her eyes watering. Just 5,000 years. Sometimes, though, she wondered if she had had too much time, and spent too much of it alone.

About the Author

Carol Scheina is a deaf speculative fiction author from the Washington, D.C., region. Many of her stories were thought up while sitting in local traffic, resulting in tales that have appeared in *Cossmass Infinities*, *Daily Science Fiction*, *Escape Pod*, and other publications. You can find more of her work at carolscheina.wordpress.com.

Demon's Blood Soup: Not Clickbait

By Avi Burton

Video thumbnail

A pink-haired man wielding a spatula and a cheeky smile. The wall behind him is painted with a pentagram made out of a red substance—possibly tomato sauce or congealed blood.

Video transcript

Welcome back to Pots, Pans, and Paranormal! I'm your host, Jace, and today we're making my great-grandmother's recipe for demon's blood soup, straight from the tome itself.

[Jace shows the audience a page from a withered book stained with black ink. The camera cuts to the countertop, where a variety of ingredients have been laid out. A black crossbow marked 'emergency use only'

is propped up against a salt shaker.]

Now, this is a surprisingly delicate soup. The demon's blood adds a sour, citrusy flavor, not unlike a yuzu fruit, so we're going to keep everything nice and light. Aside from my pre-made broth —link to that video in the description—I've got some lemongrass, ginger, scallions, peeled shrimp, and rock salt. Then, absolutely critically, we cannot forget Grandnanny's secret ingredient: crushed rose petals.

And demon's blood, obviously, but it's not a secret if it's in the video title, is it? I save the real tricks for my viewers. These are fresh rose petals culled from my garden, and all you need is just a few to make this soup taste *divine.* Or rather, demonic.

[Close up on Jace giving an exaggerated wink and finger-gun motion to the camera.]

My camera crew hates that joke, but I insisted on keeping it in the script. Anyway, we're going to let the soup base warm up and start sautéing the shrimp in butter. God, that smells delicious. Once the shrimp are done and the soup is simmering, we can add everything except the aromatics in there and focus on the main ingredient: demon's blood.

Of course, since Grandnanny couldn't make anything easy, this recipe says it has to be fresh.

[Cut to a now-cleared counter. Jace sprinkles salt in a wide circle around the edge of the stove, then cuts open his palm with a steak knife, dribbling blood on the counter. When finished, he grabs the crossbow.]

Sometimes people ask me, 'Jace, why don't you

just summon on the floor? There's so much more space!' and the answer to that, folks, is you always summon where you stir. Just basic cleanliness, really. Floors are for exorcists. We are artisans.

And now, the artistic process begins:

[Jace begins to chant. Subtitles read 'foreign language - possibly Latin?' His eyes turn black and a distant crash rattles the room. The camera quivers. Black smoke billows up from offscreen, obscuring the audience's view. When it clears, Jace has his crossbow pointed at a large red-skinned demon wearing a three-piece suit.]

Jace: Kneel before me, foul beast! Submit!

Demon: Wow, you're straightforward, aren't you? I like that.

Jace: What?

Demon: What?

[The two stare at each other in mutual confusion.]

Demon: We can save the submitting for after-dinner activities, okay? But before that, should I get to know you a little better first? Food smells delicious, by the way.

Jace: Wait—oh my God, what—

Demon: Hey, look, I know we just met, but I'd appreciate if you stopped using the G word around me. Kind of culturally insensitive.

Jace: Do you think this is a *date*?

Demon: Were the rose petals and homemade dinner not indicative of romantic intentions?

Jace: Uh.

[Jace turns towards the camera, mouthing 'what do I

do?' Camera crew's response is unclear.]

Demon: Oh, no, wait. I know what's going on here. Were you going to *kill* me? And put me in your soup? That's barbaric.

Jace: No! I—okay. That was the original plan. But you're different from what I thought. Grandnanny always said demons were heartless monsters.

Demon: You're the one aiming a crossbow at me. Do you mind putting that down?

[Jace lowers the crossbow, ashamed.]

Jace: You're right. Sorry.

Demon: I was excited when you summoned me, you know. I bought a suit.

Jace: It's not that you're not *very* attractive and all, it's just... you know.

Demon: I'm a demon and you're the heir to a line of demon hunters?

Jace: I just don't think it would work out between us.

Demon: But how will you know if you won't even give us a chance? If you go into this with a combative mindset, you've already lost.

Jace: You're very open-minded for a demon.

Demon: I'm a lawyer of hellish contracts. I read a lot, learn a lot. You know how it is.

Jace: Well-educated. I like that in a man.

Demon: And you can cook. I like *that*. What are you making?

Jace: ....shrimp soup. Care to join me?

Demon: Gladly.

[Jazzy exit music plays as the video fades out. Before

the title credits roll, the camera cuts to a new shot of Jace in a clean apron and kitchen, speaking directly to the audience.]

Remember, guys, I have new content out every Wednesday. My next one will be a storytime video: how I wined and dined a demon. Be sure to subscribe to be notified when a new video drops!

About the Author

Avi Burton (he/they) currently moonlights as a writer and daylights as a university student. He enjoys studying theater and mythology. His stories often feature queer characters, revenants, and—on occasion—laser swords. You can find more of their stories on their website, www.aviburton.com, or find the author themself on twitter under @avi_why.

BFFs

By A.D. Sui

"So, we can do like, your dead husband, or like a dead kid," the young girl says. She's wearing the most pristine baby-blue jumper. It matches her eyes. She taps the edge of her pen against a clipboard with youthful impatience. "Some people want to have a holo of their grandparent. Kind of weird, but whatever. So, what will it be?"

My feet dangle from the gurney. The patient gown is the same colour as the girl's jumper, but in cheap paper. "Can I show you?" I ask her. We don't make eye contact. She has my memories neatly projected onto a flatscreen. "Can you go to year twenty-three? July seventh, I think."

Memories flash by on the screen in a blurry mess until they screech to a halt midway through a scene of a shitty diner. Her hair was already cropped in July. She chows down her food like she's back in basic training.

"You know, we can only do dead people, right?"

the girl asks.

I know. "Don't worry about it."

We don't talk after that. The girl works quickly, with practiced precision. One electrode on my left temple and another on the back of my left ankle. "And what's her name?" she sings.

I couldn't tell her even if I wanted to. "No can do. Redaction laws."

The girl tells me there's going to be some discomfort. I hope she's right.

#

By the time I get home, it's past midnight. The girl in the baby-blue jumper said the holo should generate in a few hours. It's been six. Then again, she was always late. A terrible quality in a soldier. I slump back on my couch and wait.

I can wait; I'm good at waiting for her.

#

"I'm hungry."

I jolt awake. She's sitting on my left with the most unladylike posture, tapping along the armrest with her slender fingers. They got the hair wrong. Well, not *wrong*. They forgot the cowlick that never went away after she cut her hair short. Right at the nape of her neck.

The profile is dead on. Money well spent.

"Let's go out to eat," I say and lean over. The patch on her flight suit is blurred. Even here. They won't delete everything—that's against the law. But they will redact the shit out of it.

#

Holos are more ghosts than real people. The best science can do is extract memories; they can't create new ones. If you have the money, they'll extract as many memories as you have. I don't have that money, so I get just July 7th, 2 a.m. The woman at my side isn't sentient. She's never going to say or do anything she hasn't said or done before. But all I need is July 7th.

"I want breakfast," she says, walking slightly ahead. I used to hate scurrying along after her like this, but it's better than getting breakfast at two in the morning alone. "I know a place."

We both do. Five years of hangovers were cured here. The tables smell like coffee and bacon. I hold the door open even though she can just walk *through* it. The waitress looks at me with pity. The flight suit is a dead giveaway.

I'm dining with a holo.

#

The patch on her flight suit is blurry no matter which angle I look from.

I eat my eggs in silence. She pretends to eat her eggs. It's like watching a movie. She's not *real*. She pats the front pocket of the flight suit for a cigarette and groans with disappointment. I hand her one of mine.

"Still feel bad for introducing you to these," she

says and pretends to light up.

I don't feel bad at all. "Do you remember the day we met?"

It's weird to see someone ash a cigarette that isn't there, but no one at the diner seems to notice. "Like, the real day we met or the one you say we did?"

"The real day."

She nods, and smoke envelops her face.

#

They always make that constipated face, the one where they try to look sorry. They always wear their blues. I prefer having a regular-looking person bring me bad news than some flyboy in dress uniform.

They hand the flag over the threshold.

They never come in.

They never say they're sorry for your loss. They just stare at you with that constipated face.

"We have to implement the redaction now, ma'am," one says. The other one digs through his pocket. It doesn't hurt. They leave, and I search, and I search, and all I ever find again is INFORMATION UNAVAILABLE UNDER STATE REDACTION LAWS.

#

"Do you remember what you said to me that day?" I ask and ash my cigarette into the coffee mug.

She shrugs. "Something along the lines of *I'm so fucking high right now I can't do math?*"

The laughter bursts from my chest before I can stop it. I laugh and I laugh until I'm sobbing. "No, I mean after that." I push through the hysterical sobs.

"My name is INFORMATION UNAVAILABLE UNDER STATE REDACTION LAWS."

I'm not laughing anymore.

Even here. Two degrees of separation should have been enough. It's not *my* memory. It's a holo interacting with me. It shouldn't fall under the redaction laws.

Then I see her finger tap in rhythm.

She could never sit still, always tapping. She ashes her non-existent cigarette and winks at me.

They can censor factual information, sure. They can't censor something even I didn't know was worth censoring.

I have so many questions, but I only want the answer to one. I watch the finger tap.

Tap. Tap. Tap.

I remind myself she's not real.

But Sara, *my* Sara, was always brilliant.

We drink our coffee, and we smoke our cigarettes, and she taps on the scratched tabletop until the sun peers from behind the skyline.

About the Author

A.D. Sui is a Ukrainian-born, queer, disabled writer. She holds a Ph.D. in Health Promotion and spends most of her time being a stuffy academic of all things digital. When not writing convoluted papers that nobody will ever read, she's tweeting into the void as @TheSuiWay.

Adventures of Mmụọ

By Kasimma

Here I am o, roaming the streets of the newly dead, looking for Ned. It's hard to tell souls apart here, but I know Ned will be in the overpopulated City D. This is the fun part. To get to City D, I must travel past A through C. Such a privilege! I might as well have fun while at this. What's the worst that can happen? I'm already dead!

I stand in front of City A. I cannot walk in. There is an invisible barrier through which only those souls qualified to be in City A can cross. If I try, I will bump my head. No, I won't try. When you come here, you try if you want. They walk in twos in City A: the reincarnating soul and their Chi. These ones are set for the journey back to the Mental Plane, that place you mortals call Earth. Here, they bond tighter, waiting on a go-ahead from Chukwu. Chukwu, on the other hand, is waiting for someone to die or for

48

someone else to get pregnant so the reincarnation process will be complete. Dying is a must-do for ahụ, the humans, in the Mental Plane. Besides, they are always killing themselves. Though not compulsory, many reincarnates prefer to return to the kindred from which their soul departed. The rumor is there is a blinding hole at the end of City A from where the soul and their Chi fall through to possess the fetus whom they are to occupy in the Mental Plane.

I move on to City B. Everyone here is watching their palms or reading a book, deep-necked in research and negotiation. They are always in twos like in City A. Here, souls paired with a Chi for reincarnation strategize before their meeting with Chukwu. In that threesome meeting, the soul's destiny in the Mental Plane is settled. You only get that meeting once. There is nothing like, "I change my mind, Lord. I don't want akara again. I prefer akpụ." That is why merciful Chukwu allows you time with your assigned Chi to agree on what you want before you enter Her presence to seal your fate.

City C, my current city. I am still here because nobody in my family wants to die and release their Chi. And if there is no free Chi, how can I reincarnate? This is how they will be wasting time now until my great-great-grandson's wife gets pregnant. *Mtchew.* In City C, we walk alone; where is Chi to make us two, kwanụ? In City C, we take turns to mind the gate to the Spiritual Plane. There, we welcome the newly dead and assign judgment dates to them. C can be fun because all of us are friends.

Here is better than the Mental Plane where some senseless ahụ feels they are more ahụ than their fellow ahụ. *Ndi nzuzu*!

Well, I'm sure glad to have left City D; the overpopulated city of the newly dead. Those here are not ready for reincarnation and others have not even faced judgment. They walk in ones like us in City C. But, lord, they are almost like ahụ! They are so noisy, talking about their experiences in the Mental Plane! And now I am here because of this Ned coward.

But why would Ned run from me? Anyway, they are newcomers. They think this is the Mental Plane. Hahaha! Idiot Ned. Today, those in my set—those who died at 102—are minding the gate. How am I supposed to know that today, of all days, is Ned's death day? But you need to see the way Ned froze when they saw me and *gbalaga*! They think this is the Mental Plane. Hahaha! *Mtchew.*

But only Chukwu knows how much time I have left. Time can be tricky here. I don't want trouble. I still shudder remembering Chukwu's voice when She rebuked me earlier. What did I do? That I went to report to Her that a soul who came to my table to collect their judgment date went missing. Is reporting myself not the right thing to do?

That's how I now met Chukwu talking with Her daughter, Idemmili. I knelt. Nobody approaches Chukwu on their feet. How dare you!

"Chukwu mo!"

"Ọ gịnị?" She asked, dismissively, almost.

Chukwu was just being courteous by asking "what" because She knows everything. She is omniscient. But I answered anyway, telling Her how I had recorded the last soul's judgment date, raised my head, and Ned was next. They saw me, froze, and took off. Me? I ran in the opposite direction, to Her, to report myself or the situation or both.

That's how I now finished talking o, but She ignored me and continued Her conversation with Idemmili. Idemmili, warm as ever, gave me an assuring smile.

So (me and my big mouth) I now called, "Chukwu mo!"

She now snapped. "Ọ gịnị dị?"

I now bowed. "Lord, that I may know."

"Lord, that you may know what exactly? Lord, that you may know gịnị?"

I kept my head lowered. Chukwu's glow can blind. "Lord," I said, in all humility, "that I may know why Ned fled. Chukwu eleison!"

She laughed.

What's funny? I raised my head small.

"Ndị mmụọ a sef." She shook Her head. "Open your palm."

I obeyed. I watched Pastor Ned, wearing an oversized suit, clutching his Bible, pointing at me, screaming that if I don't give up my heathen ways, I will never make Heaven. I knotted my red lappa, laughed, and said jokingly, jokingly o, that he should bet and see, I, the so-called pagan, will be the one at Heaven's gate to judge him. And that's why Ned ran from my table here? Wonders shall never end!

Chukwu spat on the ground. "Before this spit dries, make sure you are here with my child."

That's why I'm now here o, roaming the streets of the newly dead, looking for Ned.

About the Author

Kasimma's stories and poems appear on Guernica, LitHub, Writer's Digest, Meet Cute, Native Skin, Solarpunk Magazine, The Forge Literary, The Puritan, Kikwetu, Afreecan Read, and many other journals and anthologies. She is the author of *All Shades of Iberibe* and a 2022 Nikky Finney Fellow. She's been awarded writers' residencies and workshops across Africa, Asia, and Europe. Kasimma has enjoyed, very thankfully, the privilege of learning under the voices of Wole Soyinka, Chimamanda Ngozi Adichie, and others. You can read more about her and her works on https://kasimma.com/read-online/ Kasimma is from Igboland—obodo ndị dike.

My Jam Jar Ghost

By Shih-Li Kow

I caught a ghost the other day. There were many ghosts in Mrs. Tan's house, but this was the first one I'd caught. It happened when I was reading aloud a story about a girl and a dragon to Mrs. Tan. I thought she was asleep, but she asked me to repeat the name of the girl. *Ai Ping,* I said. I looked at her and wondered if it was her who'd spoken or one of the ghosts because I'd replaced the girl's name with mine when I was reading.

Mrs. Tan's son paid me to read to her for an hour every evening. He lived down the street, but he said he couldn't stay with her himself. He said it was complicated and I wouldn't understand. So, I didn't ask why and went every day after school. Sometimes, I stayed for an extra hour or I'd put the radio on until the national anthem played at midnight. Sitting with a dying woman who never talked back was peaceful, and the ghosts never did anything more than tug at my hair on occasion. It was better than all the screaming and yelling that went on in my own house. Sometimes, I stayed the whole night. If Mrs. Tan's son saw me leave in the mornings, he never asked me why either.

The ghost I caught had floated across the room quite nonchalantly. It hung in the air—sometimes opaque, sometimes gauzy. I snagged it just as it turned white against the dark green curtains of Mrs. Tan's room. I pinched its tail and coiled it around my index finger.

It didn't look like much, this long white worm of a ghost. It didn't feel like much either. It had no weight, only a sort of damp coldness which tugged my finger like a string on a helium balloon. It was hard to believe I'd caught a ghost so easily. Collectors used all types of traps and special lights, but there were so many ghosts in Mrs. Tan's house that I suppose I shouldn't have been surprised to pluck a small one out of the air just like that.

I pressed my thumb against it to keep it from unraveling while I rummaged for something to contain it. I found a glass jar in the kitchen that looked like it would do the job. When I woke up in the morning, the ghost had wriggled into the spaces between the threads in the lid and was already half out of the jar. I pushed it back in and tightened the lid. I put the jar in a fishbowl filled with water and weighed it down with a can of sardines. I told Mrs. Tan I'd caught her a dragon and I thought I saw her smile.

My ghost didn't seem to have friends. I kept it

on Mrs. Tan's bedside table when I was reading to her, but no other ghost came looking for it. And there were many others, big and small ones that were all over the house: in the backs of cupboards and ceiling corners, under the beds, in the trees out in the garden, under the sink in the bathroom, behind every door, and even amongst the pots in the kitchen. I guessed the ghost I had must've been a bit of an outcast.

It stopped trying to escape after I put it in the fishbowl and stayed curled up at the bottom of its jam jar. If I tapped the jar, it would perk up a little. I wondered if ghosts could die if they were already dead. I wondered which made them sadder, wandering around all alone and being ignored or the attentions of a captor and a glass jar prison.

I attempted to sell it. There were people who collected these things, although mine was hardly an impressive specimen. I put up a post on eBay: *Small ghost for sale. Low maintenance.* There were two inquiries. They wanted photographs, but I didn't have the equipment to take a photograph of a ghost. It didn't show up when I used the camera on my phone. They wanted to know the exact measurements and condition of the ghost. I replied: *Approximately eight inches long. Condition is fair.* They asked for its pedigree and origin. I stopped replying. Anyway, I was getting fond of it, my first ghost.

I thought of releasing it in a place where it had friends or where there were ghosts of the same kind, but I didn't know where worm-like ghosts hung out. The black, pumpkin-faced ones liked to play under Mrs. Tan's bed and the banshees usually lounged in the trees, but I didn't know about the plain, quiet ones like the one I had. It seemed to me that my ghost might get bullied by the alpha ghosts. So, I kept it in the jar while I tried to figure out what to do.

One night, not long after I had caught the ghost, Mrs. Tan took a turn for the worse. Her every breath sounded like a drowning gasp. I called her son, the man who paid me to watch her. He came quickly and held her hand, his head bowed low. He did not see the ghost that came out of her mouth with her last breath, a white wisp approximately eight inches long.

I opened the jam jar and let my ghost out. It squirmed a little this way and that, straightening its kinks after being stuck in the jar for so long. The two of them, my ghost and Mrs. Tan's, floated towards the door together like a pair of jellyfish tentacles. A pair of dragon worms. I could've reached out and caught them both. I could've given them to Mrs. Tan's son in a jar, but it felt right just to let them be. The same way it felt right just to let the man cry.

©2022 Shih-Li Kow

About the Author

Shih-Li Kow is the author of a novel (*The Sum of*

Our Follies) and a short story collection (*Ripples and Other Stories*). Her short fiction has been published in *ParSec, Flash Fiction Online, Quarterly West,* and elsewhere. She lives in Kuala Lumpur, Malaysia. Twitter@shihlikow.

Stains of Home

By Tehnuka

The tattered carpet flaps heavily. Our pulling has given it impetus. When the end peels off, the entire strip jolts up to hover at waist-height. I grab the quivering corner, but Aunty slaps my hand.

"Don't touch!" Then, as it drifts towards the doors, she rushes to unlock them.

#

My father had the plush white cut-pile carpet laid years ago, when I was in high school.

"You grew up with cement floors," I said as the van disappeared, leaving gluey odors. "Why d'you want fancy carpet?"

"It feels nice on my feet."

He'd sit on the sofa wiggling his toes, flipping through silverfish-eaten books. I couldn't read them but knew from the covers that they were children's stories.

Aunty and I wished he'd bought fluffy socks

instead. Appa's decadence left us fearing to take cups of tea out of the kitchen. We stashed baking soda on the cubby beneath the coffee table for emergencies, to deploy tactfully when, inevitably, guests' drinks sloshed. After I spilt lentils beneath the dining table, Aunty wouldn't speak to me until I found that dish soap and arm-aching scrubbing could remove turmeric-yellow.

Appa never admitted his vanilla chai was the worst culprit. Within a week it'd formed a rusty splash where the carpet's thick edge routinely tripped him leaving the kitchen—a patch that, despite our efforts, swiftly became permanent. My complaints went unheeded. Aunty never scolded him.

#

When I returned last week, the only trace of the carpet's early brightness was a corner under the sofa where sunlight never reached. I touched the threadbare oval in front of it where Appa's heel had rubbed as his outstretched legs rocked side-to-side, one corduroy-trousered ankle crossed over the other. Sometimes he'd stop turning pages and stare right through the book, dreaming of home. Or, perhaps, recalling nightmares of youth that drove him here.

"We had it steam-cleaned," Aunty said as we sat on the floor stacking curly-scripted books into boxes. "It didn't help."

"Hardwood would've been nice," I responded.

But it wasn't the same without him to defend its softness for the umpteenth time.

With the furniture gone, we stripped the wallpaper. Then out came the utility knife, followed by pieces of the beloved carpet. The final section was not one of those few that still looked fresh, nor the vanilla-tinged part, nor that beneath the dining table printed with the history of decades in shared and lonely meals, but the near-transparent remnant where his bare feet had always rested.

Now he's gone and that last scrap, too, is going— where? In search of memories? Dreams that young feet brought when they crossed the world and, in old age, passed into its fabric? No one else had been here, ready to take them.

But I'm here now. Aunty, too. She holds the urn. It can't be a worse journey than Appa's feet made in the other direction. Chill wind blows up through the ragged carpet, but I trust it will take us home.

About the Author

Tehnuka (she/they) is a writer and volcanologist from Aotearoa New Zealand. She likes to find herself up volcanoes, down caves, and in unexpected places; everyone else, however, can find her online at tehnuka.dreamhosters.com or as @tehnuka on

Twitter, and some of her speculative stories in *Mermaids Monthly*, the *Imagine 2200* climate fiction collection, and *Worlds of Possibility*.

The Gift of Dreams

By Elizabeth Snow

"They're beautiful," the specialist said, gently turning her hand over in his own, manipulating her fingers to study the tendons beneath her skin. "The skin could use some moisture, but that's easy enough to remedy."

She smiled demurely and sighed a little. "I have a comfortable octave reach," she said. She had the hands of a pianist. That's what she'd always been told. "I never learned much more than the scales, but I've always played the children's exercises regularly." She'd had lessons as a child, and she'd loved the music. She'd been good, but they hadn't been able to afford them for long.

The specialist frowned up at her. "The prosthetic replacements *might* be dexterous enough to handle those exercises, but they'll never play anything smoothly enough to dance to."

"It's all right, really," she assured him. "We never will be able to afford lessons." If he felt she was at risk for seller's remorse, he wouldn't sign off on the procedure, and she desperately wanted him to approve it. "And anyway, we do have a radio. You know, for the dancing." She tried to smile.

He nodded. "Very well. Perhaps it's for the best after all. Holding on to dreams like that can cause its own damage."

She swallowed a lump in her throat. "Oh yes, I know that very well."

He took a deep breath and turned to grab a tablet from his desk. "All right. There's a lot of information for you to review, terms of the contract. If you're satisfied with the compensation and familiar with the process, you'll find a selection at the bottom of the document that will initiate a retinal scan. Once you agree, there's no reconsideration, so take your time." He handed her the tablet and left the room, giving her privacy for her final moment of consideration.

For all the medical advances, they still couldn't design a child before it was born. Every attempt to date had been... unfortunate. They could modify adults, however. Sculpting existing parts was always the first consideration. If the deficiency was slight enough, convenient enough, a light operation was much easier to recover from, adapt to. Whole part replacement was more common among the truly elite. Scarring was easier to hide; the finished look was more elegant. Robotic prosthetics were getting better all the time, but they lacked the grace of organic parts, and lab grown materials were still a far cry from satisfactory. The poor had been selling off their most desirable attributes through official channels and the black market for decades.

The solstice was approaching, and she desperately wanted to get her husband a gift worthy to be called a celebration of his life. They'd been together for three years, and, for once, she wanted to give him something other than cheap trinkets and day dreams.

The camera she wanted to get her husband was so expensive. With it, though, he could make something of his good eye. He could even make a career. He'd never get far with the cheap equipment they could afford, not even if they saved up for the next five years. And that number on the contract, bold, stark, back-lit by the tablet, was enough for the camera *and* a nice dinner.

They'd never be able to afford a piano, even a small, cheap one, much less the lessons she'd need...

The basic prosthetics she would get as part of the compensation package had more than enough dexterity for her weaving. The cooking, washing, and mending hardly needed more.

She shook her head, tapped the screen, and held up the tablet when prompted for the retinal scan. As she waited for the orderlies to collect her for the procedure, she found herself studying her hands like she'd never really seen them before. How long had she had that freckle? Had those veins always been so prominent? Those white spots on the nails, though, those she knew came and went in an ever-changing pattern across the brittle keratin. She wondered if she would have gotten more if her nails had been in better shape. But the orderlies came, and she was led back to a room where she was to change for the surgery.

When she got home, the camera was carefully wrapped in beautiful, crisp, silver paper. The lights were off, so she thought, for a moment, that she might have beaten him home. But when she touched the panel and lit the room, she froze halfway through the door. Her mind barely understood what she was seeing.

There, in the corner where her old out of tune keyboard used to sit, was a beautiful piano. A real piano. As she shook her head, something on the other side of the room caught her attention. Her shoulders sank when she saw the bandage wrapped around her husband's eyes.

"What have you done?" She gasped.

"Oh love," he smiled, "I don't need them for the factory. Touch and memory are more than I need. You know my purple irises were rare enough to more than cover the piano. I got enough for a year of lessons as well!"

His smile was so bright. How had it not lit the room as she'd arrived? Slowly, she crossed the room and knelt before him, carefully raising an arm to his. Hesitantly, she slid the prosthetic down to his hand and watched the confusion on his face give way to pain, the creases in his brow, the turn of his lips more than enough to convey the depths of emotion he felt.

Gently, he pulled her in close. "Well," he said thoughtfully, "I'll have to learn to play. And cameras are easy to use."

She sobbed bitterly into his arms. A piano! And lessons! She was to listen to *him* play? But he was right. Laughter punctuated her sobs. He'd had such beautiful eyes, and such an eye for beauty. They had made their choices, and they had chosen to love each other.

About the Author

Elizabeth lives with her husband, three children, and the magic cat that warns her to sit down when she has a migraine. In addition to writing, Elizabeth enjoys what she calls crafty sewing, the occasional amateur photography (so amateur she only uses her phone these days), and seasonal baking.

The Shrouded Parent in the Future

By Susan L. Lin

Congratulations! With your purchase of our His and Hers* simulation helmet bundle, you've joined 20,000** other humans in taking a collective step towards our planet's bright future! As a lucky recipient of this nascent technology, you can now travel to any of our four scintillating destinations. Looking ahead, we expect to provide additional artificial environments with every new update***, each imagined scenario more vivid than the last. Until then, we hope you and your special someone enjoy your shared foray into the great unknown!

* unlimited gender combinations and groupings available for an extra fee with our custom bundle feature
** number rounded up to the nearest ten thousand
*** additional charges will apply, naturally

I stared at the current list of options, which included "trips" to iconic eras in planetary history. Consumers could share a picnic blanket with herbivorous dinosaurs, perform a romantic skating duet during the ice age, spend an evening stargazing aboard the Titanic, or witness a live performance by their favorite band—however anachronistic—at the original 1969 Woodstock festival.

Purchasing an anniversary gift for my parents had never been easy. They were always the type to exclaim, "You shouldn't have!" as they tore away the paper to reveal the surprise hiding underneath. But their reactions weren't mere politeness—they literally meant I shouldn't have.

This time, I nervously watched as my father sliced open the box with his trusty switchblade. I kept waiting to hear them utter those familiar words, but the seconds ticked by. The disheartening exclamation never materialized.

Even so, my parents didn't look too thrilled at the prospect of a virtual vacation as they removed the device from its eco-friendly packaging. In perfect unison, they placed the interconnected helmets over their respective heads. The metallic paint and tinted visors made them look like futuristic bikers.

"It's heavy," my mother said.

"It smells like a new car," my father said.

Their voices were muffled. I couldn't see their eyes. Finally, they lifted the helmets off and placed them back in the box. They smiled at me then. "You shouldn't have, Maddie."

#

On my next visit a month later, I fully expected to find the package abandoned on a shelf, collecting dust alongside past gifts. To my surprise, the cardboard box was open on the hallway floor. It was empty.

"Mama? Baba?"

I found them in the living room. They were sitting on the couch, casually sporting the helmets as if making an avant-garde fashion statement.

"Join us!" My mother patted the seat beside her when she heard my voice. "We're feeding a triceratops scallion pancakes!"

"I'm teaching a hadrosaur how to use chopsticks!" my father exclaimed.

"You can do it, Haddie. You can do it!"

Witnessing my mother's rare excitement filled me with joy. But my elation slowly dispersed when I realized I couldn't remember a time when she'd offered me those same affirmations. I sank into the cushions and scanned the room. I tried to imagine the rug as a checkered blanket. I tried to see a teacup in place of the pen holder.

"Aw, look!" My father pointed to a floor lamp in the corner. "She's so proud of herself! Good girl! These pan-fried dumplings are delicious, aren't they? Still crispy, too!"

I looked down at my hands, a sudden void spreading throughout my stomach.

"I can't wait to watch her grow up," my father said. The shadow of a smile widened below his shielded eyes.

My mother murmured in agreement.

About the Author

Susan L. Lin is a Taiwanese American storyteller who hails from southeast Texas and holds an MFA in Writing from California College of the Arts. Her novella GOODBYE TO THE OCEAN was the winner of the 2022 Etchings Press novella prize. More of her work can be found online at https://susanllin.wordpress.com/.

The Light Will Leave You Warmer

By Taylor Rae

The metal deer is almost dead.

Willa and I are scavenging when we find it. It's maybe a quarter-mile from the house, in the tansy field that leads into the woods. It's June, and daylight gets so hot, the tansy is already brown and dead. The deer lies on its side, listless. It's been spirit-sick for weeks, and nothing I've tried has worked. My dad was a true spirit-welder. I can't even keep a goddamn deer alive.

The both of us crouch together. We wear burlap pants, belts with knives and rope, plaid jackets. We're a five-hour hike from the nearest town, deep in the woods of Old Idaho. All around us, my dad's metal songbirds flit through the trees, clicking and chirping. The scrap-animals are the only living things left out here.

"Oh, Deer-Deer," Willa says. "Don't you want to

stick around with us?"

"Don't think I can fix it this time."

"That's okay. I don't have the knack for welding *or* magic." She knocks her knee against mine and smiles, but I can't match it.

I'm already separating it in my mind—just scrap metal, just a stupid deer-ghost—because if I use its name, then it stops being junkyard magic, and it becomes the last spirit-weld my dad helped me make, and I can't fucking think about that right now. Its body is a children's bicycle frame with sheet metal ribs, jointed struts for legs. Its head is an old stop sign I hammered into shape, cutting holes for the eye sockets.

Its eyes are a weak yellow glow, like starlight.

Willa squeezes my knee. She unhooks the rope from her belt and fashions a lasso to loop around the deer's head and rusted chest.

"Let's get her home, at least," she says.

#

When I was twelve, my dad brought me into his welding workshop and showed me a delicate robin, fashioned from old soda cans. Its breast was a red Coke logo.

We can't bring the animals back, Adie. He tilted the breast-panel to show the real bird bones inside, brown with age and humming with low-frequency magic. *But their spirits are present and restless. We can give their ghosts a new shell until they're ready to pass on.*

72

Through his welder's gloves, his hands glowed, casting leonine shadows on his face. The metal robin rocked unsteadily to its feet and swayed, blinking its pinhole yellow eyes. That robin lived through another seven years of repairs, until one day it curled up and waited like a candle, hoping to burn out. My father plucked out its soul-blackened bones and buried them with a flattened soda can headstone.

Why won't you save it? I had said. *You could make its soul stay.*

For a while, he said. *But it was ready to go.*

But how do you know?

He winked. *You just do.*

#

My dad's scrap-songbirds follow us like a funeral procession. They chirp amongst each other, clicking a clever wheel Dad set in their bellies. Maybe they know Deer-Deer is dying.

Willa and I take turns pulling the rope. The deer isn't that heavy, but we're weak. We've been low on rations from the city for weeks. Willa's little garden barely grew enough to feed us for a month, even after she germinated it by hand, because I'm too clumsy to spirit-weld an army of tinfoil bees for her.

The sun hangs low and crimson when we finally reach the edge of the field, pass through a thin ribbon of forest, and enter the clearing we call home. My dad's been dead a year, and I still think of it as *Dad's house*. The old mobile home stands at the center of the clearing. My dad's workshop wilts beside it: corrugated siding gone rusty, concrete foundation sinking.

Willa pauses, panting. She nods at the workshop. "Want to bring her in to look at her?"

"And do what?" I kneel beside Deer-Deer and smooth my hand down its metal neck. Its eyes are fading but still dull yellow. "I can't make a spirit stay if it doesn't want to."

Like Dad. He was sick, but I think he also just got tired. Tired of holding on. Tired of waiting to die. When he finally went, I thought about putting his bones in a metal shell and seeing what opened its yellow eyes and looked back at me.

Deer-Deer's eyes are winking out like a match, burning low. Its face is so dented and dead already. How did my dad ever make this sad hunk of metal look alive? How will I ever do it again without him?

Willa tilts her head toward the forest and smiles, tiredly. "At least all her friends came to the funeral."

I follow her stare. Dozens of my dad's birds are gathered on tree limbs and fence posts, on bushes and brambles. But there are more eyes, too, glowing in the twilight.

There's the bear my dad reconstructed from a pair of scrapped Gold Wings, the exhaust pipes sticking out from its elbows. There's the first animal I ever made—a fox with a crooked face and mismatched eyes. There's Deer-Deer's buddy, Elk-Elk, who's so huge its eyes look like twin moons. Even our housecat, a cranky spigot with a metal teapot head, has joined the observers.

I can almost imagine my dad's ghost beside them, clear as moonlight and just as bright.

Deer-Deer's chest is still hot when I reach between its metal ribs. I pluck out its bones, one by one. They're so blackened, they almost ash apart in my hands.

But Deer-Deer's spirit hums in those bones. It's still humming when Willa digs a hole beside my father and his little metal robin. It's still humming when I press the bones into the earth, all my dad's metal animals haloing around us.

We stand among our ghosts and pray the only way we know how: laughing, retelling stories, and hoping the spirits we've lost can hear us.

About the Author

Taylor Rae is a professional cave troll, hidden away in the mountains of Coeur d'Alene, Idaho. She likes avoiding her neighbors, playing ukulele, and longboarding. Most of her stories involve spaceships and/or magic. She is the winner of the 2021 NYC Midnight Short Story Contest, and her work appears with *Flash Fiction Online*, *PseudoPod*, and *Fit for the Gods* from Vintage Books. More at www.mostlytaylor.com.

The Care Giver

By Frances Ogamba

Sam always bangs the mortuary door with an iron rod before twisting the knob. He asks if he can come in. A gale hits him. A collective yawn. He nudges the door wider, beaming, happy to meet his friends again. He reels out their names from the entrance. Mary, the bulky fifty-year-old, of pallet number thirty-five, never hears him on time. Sam overhears her clambering back into her hulk, her whispered cusses bouncing off the walls. There is Odika too, formerly deaf, who scurries about the room for a full minute before settling into his body.

Located at the edge of an expressway, the morgue is foreran by dense shrubs and cashew trees. The community built it as a spot to receive accident victims. Now, it serves everyone—the poisoned, the sick, the murdered. Sometimes, they spill onto the expressway, wrangling over trivial issues. The natives of the community would lodge a complaint to their chief and Chief would lodge a complaint to Sam.

While dressing them the first time, Sam makes an incision near the clavicle and drains out blood, asking if anyone knows a thing that goes up empty-handed and comes down with water. When he gets no answer, he chants: coconut! What walks into the bush clapping? he asks next. He believes he hears an answer whispered over the damp air of the hall. Ukpaka! Oil bean! It could be from a Paul or a Felix. They gurgle in satisfaction as he claps for them.

The job pays a paltry sum. Sam hangs on to it while looking for a new job. But his rough edges are already smoothed out. He holds authority over this large room of roughly six hundred bodies. About twenty or more come in daily, recoiling from his touch as he washes and towels them dry. He removes excess gas from cavities and sutures cuts closed. He tempers their rage when it froths, and plays guide and guard until families come to take them home. Sam's favourite rite is dressing them up for the funeral. The clasping of jewelry around necks and wrists. Pushing earrings into earlobe holes. Clipping fingernails and toenails. Heaping foundation on faces to conceal damages or lighten the darkening effect of chemicals. Sketching eyebrows. Light painting of eyelids. Bronzer powder to lift the nose.

He takes messages for their loved ones too.

Tell my wife my ATM pin is the same as my phone password. This is the address of the landed property I have at Ugwuoba. Tell my mum that Uduji poisoned me. Tell her. She will understand. Please let my little girl know Daddy never wanted to leave.

Sam is the first to unveil them, ripping jewelry and expensive clothes off bloodied and limp bodies. Medical doctor. Keke rider. Professor of Languages and Literatures. A lab technician. Special Adviser to some Governor. They come to Sam the same.

A family arrives one night as Sam prepares to switch off the lights, depositing their brother who had an accident. Only the lady among them is able to answer Sam's questions as he makes entry. The dead man's face is creased as if he was rudely disrupted during an important speech. His forehead remains furrowed even though it happened over seven hours ago.

When the family leaves, Sam bends to retrieve the man's shoes. A voice chides him, "Hey! Mister! Careful with those shoes! They are new!"

Sam jumps back. All the bodies he has tended speak in undertones that often get lost if he does not pay attention. But this man's voice is as clear as one who sits amongst the living.

Sam shrugs off the fear prickling his skin like a burn. He knows the words to use. The angriest of them always succumbs to the purl of his voice. He places a hand on the man's chest.

"Brother, I am so sorry this happened to you.

I know it hurts, but be a little patient so I may clean your wounds and sew you whole." Sam feels the eyes of the others feasting on him and the newcomer.

"Brother, I need to unbutton your suit now. This is quite an expensive suit. I would love to own something like this."

A little stir.

"As if you can afford it. You will need four more jobs to be able to. Hand it over to my siblings."

His words slam Sam in the gut and stir a little vexation. Still, he understands the man's state is what fuels his waspish tongue. He imagines being on the way to work and his destination suddenly swapped, placing him on the way to elsewhere. What to do with unfinished projects? How does anyone reconcile with such a sudden interruption?

"Sorry brother." Sam reassures him, anchoring himself against further onslaught.

They continue like that; the man cussing and Sam imploring and undressing until the man lies naked on his pallet.

When Sam goes home that night, he sleeps poorly. The man's words prod him into the tangled forest of his life. The misery of toiling so hard and getting so little in return. A low twang of sadness spreads through him like shrapnel.

In the morning, Sam, still burdened, bounds through the door without knocking. In the myths, anyone who walks through such doors without warning sees the dead souls in their truest forms. There are stories of torture. Limbs or heads hewn off in fury. But what Sam walks into is thick darkness. Rooms within rooms. The pallets formerly holding the corpses now transform to one-winged trees. Walls shift and birth new hallways and streets and a town holding all the bodies Sam has ever washed. They appear pink and full, reeking of Sam's formaldehyde. They speak to Sam as if he has always belonged here.

When some members of the community, frayed by worry over Sam's whereabouts, arrive at the morgue after two days, they find an unattended hallway of bodies.

©2022 Frances Ogamba

About the Author

Frances Ogamba is a 2022 CLA fellow at the University of Minnesota, Twin Cities. A winner of the 2020 Kalahari Short Story Competition and the 2019 Koffi Addo Prize for Creative Nonfiction, she is also a finalist for the 2019 Writivism Short Story Prize and 2019 Brittle Paper Awards for short fiction. Her fiction appears or is forthcoming on *Ambit, Ninth Letter, Chestnut Review, CRAFT, New Orleans Review, Vestal Review, The Dark Magazine,*

Uncharted, midnight & indigo, Jalada Africa, in The Best of World SF Vol. 2 and elsewhere. She is a 2022 Pushcart Prize Nominee and her stories have been recommended on must-read lists by Tor Magazine. She is an alumna of the Purple Hibiscus Creative Writing Workshop taught by Chimamanda Adichie.

Terran Holiday

By Alison Tam

Contrary to expectation, the first thing I felt when I stepped off the shuttle to Terra was not a full-body flashback to an ancestral memory of the first hominids. It was hangover heaviness, post-family dinner bloat, every single part of my body holding a passive protest against standing up.

We were weighed down by a truly disgusting amount of gravity, the authentic experience we expected when we bought tickets for an all-inclusive, reasonably-priced Terran Extravaganza. Our package tour promised to run through humanity's greatest hits in two days and three nights: Pyramids, Great Wall, Machu Picchu, then home before the weekend ended.

I'd gone full lunar stereotype. Orbit drones circled around me, a pouch pack on either hip and a concussion-preventing puffer helmet strapped to my delicate little dome. I even hesitated when taking my first step off-ship, scared of getting injured before I got my first whiff of Terran dirt. I raised one foot, tilted forward... and instantly slammed down, impact rattling through my bones.

All the cool Earth facts in the galaxy couldn't prepare me for feeling gravity's pull, time cruelly accelerating just to make me fall faster. Every single step on this planet would be the same. I had never, ever felt so heavy.

#

My skin dried out immediately on contact with Cairo's desert air. Terrans can air-condition as much as they want, but Earth doesn't have humidity control. We trundled through traffic jams as holograms of kushari and falafel tempted us from the street, chess cafes so close that we could play a match from the window.

When we caught our first glimpse of a pyramid, a great involuntary *ooh* rose from us as one. We blinked open our retinal imagers and snapped photographs.

The gift shop and bathrooms ruined the shot, but we weren't really trying to get a good picture. There are taller buildings back home, our own great monuments to cricket and pop music, but this was real history. We were trying to capture the feeling of hot sun and dry air, each having our own private epiphany about what it meant to be standing here.

"My people built that," said my seatmate. "I'd never seen it before."

I had a joke prepared, something cynical about

the working conditions of the time period, but at the genuine wonder on her face, it died, ashamed, on my tongue.

She felt a connection to this land, an ownership, a lineage spanning the breadth of human history. Next to it, all my studied quips were nothing. She may have had the lunar look, ashy skin and elongated limbs, but in that moment, there was something in her that belonged to Earth.

#

We shuttled off to see the Great Wall the day after. For a little extra I could've come on a flight with an orbital view, but I hadn't bothered to shell out for the premium package.

What an arrogant sentiment, to think that culture can be had for a weekend on the cheap. The sheer optimism shatters me. Maybe it's because we all watched Blue Planet when we were kids. Pekoe thrived in the same tropical waters as her long-lost relatives, accepted despite the divergence of diaspora and her inability to swim. We've seen the ads, the essays, the university study abroad brochures. There is a Terran industrial complex, dedicated to selling the fantasy of Earth.

In the land my ancestors called home, I walked the stones of their greatest monument and took a photograph of myself with my arms spread out, pretending to hold up half the sky.

"It really is amazing," I said, and felt nothing.

I'd wanted the idea of Earth so very badly.

I wanted resonance, recognition, *terra cognita*. Instead, I was Chinese by way of Luna by way of Toronto by way of Singapore, each successive wave of ancestral immigration taking me further from what could have been my home.

#

There was precipitation on the last day of our trip, and we didn't even get an alert. The heavens simply dispensed water with no regard to the travelers in their midst, an entire precious deluge used for nothing but drenching our clothes.

Everything on Luna is meant for our use. We are the center of our own constructed ecosystem, a vast machine dedicated to ensuring we're fed, hydrated and sufficiently entertained. We treat Terra like one of our resources, attempting to allocate meaning like we do oxygen, but like everything else on the planet, Earth's culture defies control. I imagine Terrans must live their lives in perpetual surrender, always subject to their own atmosphere's whims.

Maybe that's what they know about history, and we don't. Instead of trying to plumb the depths of the past for sentiment, they live their lives around it and let emotion fall upon them like rain.

I hauled myself slowly up the stairs of Machu Picchu alone, far behind the rest of my tour. The rain had stopped, but the stone beneath me was slick, the steep descent below promising worse than broken bones. I sat down to rest and hyperventilate, clinging to the steps.

A cluster of tourists conversed quietly in Mandarin's tongue-curling tones as they passed me. I am sure I was as alien to them as they were to me, the two of us made mutually unintelligible by the waves of migration that had washed away my heritage.

But the shape of our eyes, the dark oil-shine of our hair, the scolding tone a mother used to force her child into standing up straight—those were the same.

Suddenly I could picture the ancestors I had failed to see at the Great Wall. Not emperors or laborers but travelers like myself, in search of something they could not name. At last I felt the importance I had come here to find, the kinship, the heritage. The weight of generations, pulling us like gravity inexorably to the earth.

About the Author

Alison Tam is a queer Taiwanese-American writer, reader and lifelong diaspora dreamer. She likes thinking about ordinary people living in extraordinary worlds. She's written everything from cyberpunk tabletop RPG settings to giddy romantic comedies about swordswomen who love high femmes. Find her on alisontam.github.io or on twitter.com/thetamslam.

Pearlskin, Or the Oysterman's Wife

By Elou Carroll

Euan's wife is in the bathtub—is always in the bathtub. Surrounded on all sides by salt-bucket sentinels. The water laps over the rim as she rises to snatch up a trowel of sea salt. Pearlskin tips it into the ice-cold bathwater, presses the wrinkled pad of her finger to the trowel to collect any errant grains and shoves them in her mouth. Then, she sinks back beneath the surface, eyes open, lips bobbing wide.

The Oysterman closes his eyes and the door, but his resolve ebbs and flows like a tide—and the tide is currently out. Seeing her this way feels like voyeurism, like trespass, but it is the only way he can. Euan, who has not bathed in days, still smells like the sea and when he steps into the bathroom, she emerges at the scent, her wet head cresting the water so only her eyes are visible over the tub.

The Oysterman's wife looks at him as if she wants

to kiss him or curse him, kill him or crawl inside him and curl up into the shell of his spine.

#

Euan had never intended to dredge himself a bride—when the net refused to rise to the schooner, he'd thought it caught on a rock or somesuch. He let the boat swivel starboard, tried the crank again and with a good swift tug, pulled the haul aboard. It wasn't the netful of oysters he'd been expecting, no, but one large oyster shell, about as big as a child's paddling pool.

"Ain't that something." Jim whistled between his teeth. A friend of his father's, Jim was there more for company than help. The old man hobbled forward. "Never seen nothing like it."

Euan wet his lips. "Stand back, Jim."

The Oysterman slid a large knife into the lip of the oyster. The shucking was slow-going, but with each deft movement, the shell began to yield. It opened with a pop and a crunch, and there, inside the shell, nestled into the wet flesh of the oyster, was a woman curled up tight like a chiton.

"I'll be," said Jim, swiping the hat from his head and holding it to his chest. The woman in the shell shivered and, where the crisp sea air touched her, her skin began to harden. Pearlskin's mouth opened in a soundless wail and the clouds above darkened and swirled and loomed over the schooner like the fist of God. "Come on, lad. Best get to shore and quick. There's a foul mood upon the wind."

"What about the—"

"No time for that. We'll bring it with us."

Euan shoved the shell closed and made for the port, covering the oyster with a thick blue tarp. He tried not to notice the way the cloudhead calmed —only for a moment—until there came a noise like scratching, clawing to get out, muffled by shell and thick plastic. Then, he tried not to notice how the clouds followed.

By the time they'd hefted the shell home, the woman was near-completely solid—only her frantic eyes darted and the tips of her fingers twitched. It was then they dropped her in the bathtub, hardened pearl clanging against tin. She softened some with the water but soon began to wither and choke.

"Salt," said Jim. "Get her some salt."

#

When Euan looks into the water, he sees her skin dance with light and wants to touch it. Instead, he lifts a bucket and pours a quart of salt into the tub. Pearlskin closes her eyes and leans back, baring her throat to him, and something in his stomach clenches. His teeth clamp on his bottom lip and he leaves her, white knuckled, to her bath.

Outside, wind batters the windows. It is hard to walk against the ocean's shouting breath.

The bay has been stormful ever since the Oysterman plucked his wife from the seabed. The fish market packed up, the general store shut its doors, even the post office hung a CLOSED *(indefinitely)* sign in its window, hidden now by thick planks of wood, desperate protection from the angry sea. The only place still running—always running come rain, shine or war—was the ANCHOR'S END public house. There, Euan listens to old fishermen talk of a curse upon the port.

"There's something evil in it," they say. "Something rotten. Someone's taken what the sea ain't want to give."

#

He tells himself he doesn't want her as he battles his way back to the house—that he can throw her back, easy as fishing, just like that, and he could until he sees her. Until her eyes, so pale, meet his. Until her eyelids close and her lips part just so.

"One kiss," Euan whispers to himself. "One kiss and then it's the sea with her. A husband deserves as much."

But Euan has never been a husband, not really, and the sea has never truly been his wife.

Pearlskin holds a hand out to him, and the Oysterman takes it. He lets her pull his hand beneath the water until it is covered up to his wrist—he wouldn't want her to harden, to ossify out here in the dry.

The sea reaches up with roving fingers, salt-sharp talons clawing up the Oysterman's house. The window pane cracks, but Euan does not notice. Outside, the gale and the waves take the port in their storm-clad fists—

Just one kiss—he tells himself and lets her pull him into the bathwater. She would like him better there, where it's wet, and what is a husband to do but please his wife? One kiss, here, and then to the sea. The Oysterman smiles as she opens her mouth, smiles as she shows him her teeth.

—and squeeze.

About the Author

Elou Carroll is a graphic designer and freelance photographer who writes. Her work appears or is forthcoming in *Hexagon SF Magazine*, *Apparition Lit*, *Underland Arcana*, *Kaleidotrope*, *In Somnio: A Collection of Modern Gothic Horror* (Tenebrous Press), *Spirit Machine* (Air and Nothingness Press), *Ghostlore* (Alternative Stories Podcast) and others. When she's not whispering with ghosts, she can be found editing *Crow & Cross Keys*, where she publishes all things dark and lovely, and spending far too much time on twitter (@keychild). She keeps a catalogue of her weird little wordcreatures on www.eloucarroll.com.

The Xephalopod

By Murtaza Mohsin

"Papa, he's too old," I whined again.

My father's eyes narrowed. *A man of faith and certainties worries less,* he likes to tell me. When you spend a lifetime in cold, automated submarines, waiting for commands that don't make sense, he knows best. "Orders are orders, especially for cannon fodder." Words you could live by on the *GNS Cygnus.*

"But Johnny's too slow; he'll never make it past the first barrier reef, much less get close to the target." The old Xep and I took a long, steady look at my father together.

Dipping my hand in the tepid water of the holding pod, I splashed it against Johnny's mantle. It'll be cold when we flood the torpedo tube. Suddenly, Johnny's tentacles scrambled for me as if he's panicking like some youngling pod. Of course, he knew what was happening, what was expected of him... We are at war with the wily and stubborn

Hssin. They are an island nation, a string of pearls strung across the oceans, which must be defeated and subsumed like many before them. The octopus squadrons are now "an integral component of our empire's red-ocean war strategy" according to the communiques.

Johnny senses the absence of squadron members who've departed before him. I tried to protect him, but there's always a bottom to the barrel. And he's a Xephalopod, bred for war, weaving past traps and obstacles, armed with high-order cognitive behavioral adaption. My father stared at the sonar for anyone sneaking up on us. For the hundredth time, his beady eyes traced the target coordinates and waypoints shared by Command. His movements were brisk, perhaps happy to steer home to receive a new Xep squadron to replace the one we had expended.

Ignoring my wheedling, he pushed the harness towards me with steady, heavy hands. The black bulk surprised me. Off went the IR strobe and vid-feed—unnecessary bulk for a non-reconnaissance mission. With room freed, I slapped on black kontact explosive bricks. Their dark menace chilled me. How could even the rich and powerful Hssin resist when we had a thinking munition that could actively interrogate its environment, delivering its payload regardless of its own demise?

By now, Johnny's tentacles were restlessly twitching. My father tried to massage each sinuous extension with gentle forbearance. Just like the old manuals; "to calm the beast down." He's always oblivious to the fact it doesn't always elicit the desired response. Moving quickly, I lowered myself into the holding pod to my chest and placed my face against one slit-like eye so that I was all Johnny could see. His slick form felt tight against my overalls. Johnny slowly calmed as his suckers relaxed. Behind me, my father retreated quietly before he tripped on a push trolley stretching for the release valve.

The water was no gentle swelling; the propellant tube rapidly flooded with seaweed and flotsam—we were close to the ocean's surface.

Johnny had become oddly passive.

Perhaps our ministrations had worked, but I've always thought they're not actually meant for the Xeps. In truth, these rituals mean nothing to them and are designed primarily to dull the minds of submarine crews with familiar routines. I felt a cold, numbing comfort in my father's presence with his broad back turned towards me, intently studying the sonar.

"It's nearly over now, friend." It is for me anyway, to be brutally honest. Despite my best effort to dedicate myself fully to the end of my friend's existence, I couldn't help but think of warm breezes on the fraying pier and seagulls. We pulled up the cradle that would speed him out of the sub. Our obedient old Xep probed the cradle before gingerly contorting his body to snugly fit inside. I sighed; this is the way of the world.

My father started his countdown. Surely, there's still time to take up the tip of Johnny's tentacle and run my fingers down the envelope, stimulating the neurons nestled inside. As if in response, a tentacle gently alighted at the edge of the old, faded cradle to which new, gleaming red propellant charges were attached. Slowly, Johnny was being maneuvered to position by a gentle current. My father was saying something, but I ignored him. *Just trying to say goodbye to my friend, Dad.* At least let me do that.

I looked to the chronometer's silver glow over the hatch. His tentacles lashed outwards for my hand, and I felt pain anew. The time for affection had passed. I tried to bat him away, but Johnny was relentless, those gentle suckers slowly fixing me.

So close to the hatch, I knelt and shivered in my damp overalls, hearing the sizzle of dried eggs. My stomach contracted in anticipation. We'll have fresh omelette today, just like on any other launch day.

But Johnny's grip was tighter now, remorselessly firm. His left violet iris violently expanded and contracted. I became entranced by the universe within them. Seething, waiting to be born. My hand was sharply pinned by his black, mysterious beak before he bit deeply. I tried to scream, but the paralyzing poison in his maw was much too fast for me. It's what Johnny uses against nosy combat divers. I tried to shift my head toward dad. As always, his unblinking gaze would be fixed on the sonar before firing.

Sirens exploded to life as the world dissolved

into a deep, unforgiving green. First my head, then my body tumbled into the water. The xephalopod weapon system was finally engaged. The last thing I heard before the mad rush was the bellow of a wounded animal. My father was screaming hysterically, but it seemed impossibly far away as I drifted off in Johnny's firm but tender grasp. Johnny could never have let us part so easily.

About the Author

Murtaza Mohsin is a writer from Lahore, Pakistan. His fiction also appears or is forthcoming in *Diabolical Plots*, *Galaxy's Edge*, *Future SF Digest* and *Tasavvurnama*. He can be reached via Twitter @murtazamohsin4

Come Away from the Fire, My Love

By Jenna Hanchey

In the third season of fire, the air thickened, choking off even my will to hold you. A will that had persisted, outpacing material circumstances, stretching far longer than our stores of supplies. A will that finally broke the day I stood upon the ramparts and watched the lightly falling flakes. It transported me back to our childhood, when you would create snownymphs and spin tales of their adventures in faraway lands. Before you had read all the books on elementals in the library, before you learned to speak to them.

Before you became like them.

I opened my mouth that day, like you used to. Giving into fancy, for a moment.

Instead of cool relief, my tongue netted only ash.

It tasted of grief. Yours or mine, I could not tell. Perhaps the two were inextricable. At that moment,

I knew it was over.

I watched your flames stretch over the mountainside, reaching high into the air. Frantic slashes, wrestling against the inescapable grasp of the earth. You were attempting to pull away, I finally realized. To be free.

You had made your choice long ago. And it was not me.

In the third season of fire, I let you go.

#

In the second season of fire, the kingdom of Arythe was cut off from the seas, marooning many on the wrong side of the pass. Arytheins, unable to bring the bounty of the ocean home. Seadwellers, unable to reach their shores. You'd done this on purpose. Wielded your wings of flame to scourge the mountains, hurting them as a proxy for me. How selfish of you! To take out your pain on innocent trees and creatures. If you suffered, the fault was your own. You were alone out there in the wilds, just as you'd been alone when you left me to seek the spirit realm. Had you only stayed with me in the castle, I would have cared for you. Given you everything you needed.

I only needed you. Why couldn't you understand that?

In the second season of fire, I held tighter.

#

In the first season of fire, flames danced high

in the mountains. I watched, in awe of you and of myself. I thought it beautiful, the twirling and twisting color. Your new form, still touching the plane of the fire nymphs, yet re-tethered to the kingdom—thanks to me. Years I had searched for the spell that could pull you back from the spirit realm. You never said so, but I knew you were waiting. Anticipating. And now you showed your gratitude by making the light laugh, gurgling with delight at the very edge of my kingdom.

As far as you could now go from me.

And yet I could not reach you. The forest burned, but I was too far away to feel the heat. Still I grew warm, reveling in the spurts of blue and white cresting the ridgeline, even if their intensity felt out of place in that joyful moment. Too hot, your jagged flames cut the landscape. Sharp enough to draw blood.

Perhaps the ends matched the means. After all, blood soaked the tower where I'd practiced the magics necessary to snatch you away from the fire nymphs.

It was worth it. I succeeded.

In the first season of fire, I brought you home to me.

#

Before the seasons of fire, before the spring that finally broke them, came the spring that broke me. *You* broke me.

How could you? You knew how much I needed

you. How I turned to you every time a decision needed to be made, how I leaned on your emotional wisdom and intuition. How I relied on your knowledge of other lands and peoples, your long days in the library and easy conversation with visitors. You took that from me! Even knowing I had little time for study, little understanding of empathy, little grasp on implications, you abandoned me.

Even knowing I loved you.

I had always loved you, from the easy days of play in the snow. I wanted you by my side forever. I needed you. And as King, I should have had you.

As subject, as friend, as lover, you should have acquiesced.

You knew what kind of a King I would be without you.

It was raining the day before you fled the castle. A fine spring morning, warmer than usual. It was thought to herald heavy blooms to come. I found you in the library, unsurprisingly. You must have heard me come in, but you continued to stare at the low blaze flickering in the fireplace.

"Have you made your decision?" Longing made my voice tight.

"I have."

I waited for more. It would be undignified to ask again. When you finally turned toward me, your face was answer enough.

I was the one who turned away then, hands gripping the windowsill as the rain pounded down in time with my furious heart.

"You will always be my King." Your words were heavy with feeling, but not with the one I sought. "But I cannot stay. My place is not here, kept inside, apart from the world. I have so much to learn!" You pointed at the open book in your hands. "Did you know we once traded with the elementals? We sent ambassadors to air, water, earth, and fire. We could do so again! Imagine what that would do for your reign!" The excitement in your voice cut.

A single word was all I could manage. "No."

"But I know how to reach them, how to speak the language of fire! I know it will change me, but I'm willing to accept the price in order to learn. To see the world from a different plane, can you imagine?"

"No." I did not look at you.

I looked at the rain, beating the ground into submission.

The impact rattled as you slammed the door—to the library, to a life with me—shut.

Before the seasons of fire, you left.

About the Author

Jenna Hanchey has been an actress, particle physicist, Peace Corps volunteer, and afterschool-space-program teacher, and is currently a professor of critical/cultural studies at Arizona State

University. Her stories appear in *Nature:Futures*, *Daily Science Fiction*, *Medusa Tales*, *Wyngraf,* and *Martian Magazine*, among other venues. Having once been called a "badass fairy," she attempts to live up to the title. Follow her adventures on Twitter (@jennahanchey) or at www.jennahanchey.com.

Do You Understand the Words that are Coming Out of My Mouth?

By Wen Wen Yang

The new Polyglot Earbuds actually had my parents' language as a translation option. My cousins said it was too cheap to be good. I bought them as soon as I had saved enough.

When I say I don't know yu jiu wu, I mean my tongue and brain don't like to work together. It's called *receptive bilingualism*. I understand, but I can't produce.

I tried learning Mandarin for four years in college, but the sounds are just different enough that it didn't work.

The implant was an outpatient procedure, and I spent a long weekend recovering on the couch. I caught up on a sitcom about a Chinese American family. It had gotten some criticism last year when it was announced. None of the writers, producers, or directors had been Asian. Still weren't.

There was an episode where the adult characters got drunk at a bar and the makeup department didn't even redden their faces. They wore shoes in the house! I found more issues with the show as I recovered. I eventually gave up and watched a British murder mystery.

The next weekend, I practiced with my cousins first. They filled my tiny apartment   with char siu, bok choy, and egg tarts.

I thought of my next sentence in English, then waited for the implant to translate. The earbud fed me the sounds. My tongue still struggled to replicate them.

"You installed a Turing test," they teased, staring at the healing wound behind my ear.

"I am *barely* a cyborg." They had insulin pumps and cochlear implants.

"Are you even Chinese when you aren't wearing it?"

My cousins know my soft spots.

But a month later, while I was struggling to chew through some zongzi, I tried speaking to my grandparents.

My grandmother laughed, covering her mouth.

"Your yu jiu wu has gotten so good. You should visit more often." She placed another slice of braised tofu and mushroom on my plate. It was like the goddess Kuan Yin herself was smiling at me with a dyed black perm.

After a year, I was finishing sentences before the translation software was done. I sometimes switched to Cantonese or Mandarin, just to listen to the different tongues.

Then one day, my cousin Michelle sent me a text "OMG it's us!" with clip from the show I had watched during my recovery.

It *was* us. These actors reenacted our previous Lunar New Year dinner where my uncle's employee was a complete—well, he hit on my seventeen-year-old niece. Then barfed at the table. Uncle fired him as soon as he sobered up. So he'd remember.

Jeez, did that many men barf to welcome in the new year? Or did the show have cameras in the restaurant? I watched other clips, and it felt like déjà vu. The uncle who always needed to borrow money, the aunt who talked about your weight when you weren't in the room, then poured more food onto your plate.

I dived deep into the show's social media, even the production crew's information. Maybe one of the actors saw our dinner. Then I recognized that one of the director's spouse's surnames was the same as the translation software used in the Polyglots. I sent the device's terms and conditions back to Michelle because she's a lawyer.

"It's in the T&C that they can use recordings from the earbuds for research purposes," she replied. "Get those things out of your head."

Nobody read that! I had sold access to my life for more access to my family.

I was madder than when my grandma lost a fight over a restaurant bill. I wrote a thread and tagged everyone on the show and the manufacturer. It was the first time I went viral. Hopefully, the last.

One person got ratioed. *"Paranoid much? Don't you want representation? You people are never happy."*

Then the writers and manufacturers replied.

"We aimed for an authentic voice." They thought stealing our stories was fair.

For the next dinner with Grandma, I left the earbuds at home. I won't lie. I stumbled through the conversation. But our jokes, our intimacy, would stay around the dining table.

Until Grandma had her morning gossip calls.

About the Author

Wen Wen Yang is a first generation Chinese American, raised in the Bronx, New York. She graduated from Barnard College, Columbia University with a degree in English, Creative Writing. You can find her fiction in *Fantasy Magazine*, *The Arcanist*, *Factor Four Magazine* and forthcoming in *Zooscape* and the anthology "Fit for the Gods." She tweets @muteddragon and updates WenWenWrites.com.

The Muse Dies in This One (Again)

By Kelly Piggott

She is the mother and your protagonist smothers her with a pillow in her sleep for all of the nights she beat you. She used the same belt her father beat her with and told you it was for your own good, that this was what she was dealt and look how good she turned out? You take her twelve-year-old daughter's hands and press the pillow over her face until she stops struggling and you press her twelve-year-old daughter's knee into her chest to keep her down. She dies.

Dead Mom Thirty-Two.

#

She is the woman with chestnut hair that falls over her shoulders in waves with perfectly coiffed curls and pursed lips that are curved to resemble the center of a rose a lily a daffodil a whatever-the-fuck flower. Your hard-boiled detective investigator rogue cop desires and hates her as her corpse is dug up from the ditch where unspeakable acts were committed and you tease the reader about the circumstances of her death. She's been missing for two weeks, and her chest cavity has burst open.

Dead Missing-Now-Found White Woman Sixty-Seven.

#

She is the waif bedside nurse in the war infirmary. The daughter of a general a colonel a commander the bookshop keeper the lonely wife of a man gone off to war, who has gone cold and disaffected and doesn't answer her letters anymore. The bombs are falling and her lips are as red as the propaganda posters and your young nubile virginal soldier boy indulges in a single night of passion before he goes off to battle. She's crushed in the infirmary when it's bombed.

Dead Historical Fiction Romance Period Drama Love Interest Number Twenty-One.

#

She is the girl who pulls your small town repressed depressed and wet college freshman girl protagonist into her dorm room while the party drones on with shitty pop music. Spilled cheap piss beer stuck to the carpet whose stains they'll scrub out until the fabric rips up and smell of weed smoking over heads and sweaty bodies. She takes your girl protagonist's hands to her breasts and says come on it's just practice for later and she kisses your girl protagonist and brings her mouth down. This continues for three months before the girl from the party decides she has never met your girl protagonist in her life and calls her a stalkerish lezzy freak. Your girl protagonist never forgets about her and finds out she dies off-page at age thirty from binge drinking. Unhappy and alone in a marriage as unsatisfying as your girl protagonist's love life is confused and messy from too much drinking and bad sex.

Dead Questionably Straight Girl Number Thirteen.

#

She dies from a drug overdose. She drowns in the river after having gone mad and her dress is as white as she would wear at the wedding your protagonist never got to attend. She dies offscreen in a car accident to remain a ghost and a traumatic bruise on your child narrator's brain he can't ever forget and he resents and wants her back each day. She's murdered and stuffed in a box delivered to your CIA member's doorstep by the serial killer he's been stalking for months and this is his hero's journey and his slow descent into depravity. She dies in a ritual sacrifice in the basement of a fraternity house as a demon claws its way out of the mess of blood and open-gored flesh to peer upon the boys hungry for money fame sex and notoriety who your urban fantasy protagonist has to stop at all cost. She is the sister of your protagonist who envies and loves and loathes and wants to be her all at once and she dies by her boyfriend's hands before your protagonist can help her escape.

She is your mother your sister your lover and your almost lover and you hate her and love her and want to save her and you can't stop killing her. You have killed her in over three hundred drafts.

#

"Fuck it. I've had enough."

The Muse steps out of the notebooks and closed laptop, her limbs snapping into place with the smack of a nail clipper clamp clicking closed. She shoves on your sweatpants that you've abandoned for old, worn-out underwear and a cami from the pile of clothes in the corner—your depression pile. Your vibrator and a bottle of lube sit amongst the wrinkled pile. The Muse flicks up a bra you haven't worn in weeks and toes a sweater. With her foot, she tosses it up and throws it on.

Blood crusts along her mouth, bruised at the corner, and she scoffs while wiping it off with a thumb. She takes your cold cup of coffee and perks a thick-thin-nonexistent eyebrow on her forehead. Her face changes with each blink: files on a projector.

"I'm starting to wonder if you actually like me or not. This repression shit is just not doing it for me anymore."

Her face gets stuck between two different masks:

one of your hot and cold lover and your own face. It stops in place and the Muse leans forward as if to kiss. The coffee smells dry and crisp on her lips. She cups your face as your lover does and the Muse has the same scar on her index finger as yours from the wine glass you gripped too tight at the bar the night you met your lover. The Muse's face is caught mid-change and her mouth is your lover's and her nose is your mother's and her eyes are yours.

The Muse's hands brace around your neck.

"Let's make a deal. Why don't we both live in the next one?"

©2022 Kelly Piggott

About the Author

Kelly Piggott (she/her) is a lesbian writer and teacher from the Midwest. A graduate of the MFA program at Georgia College and State University, she writes about bodies, shame, complicated relationships, and obsesses over folk and fairy tales. Her writing can be found with *Impossible Archetype*, *Body Parts Magazine*, and forthcoming with others. She currently lives in Atlanta, Georgia and can be found on Twitter and Instagram @kellbellhells.

You, A Shield of Glaze

By Lark Morgan Lu

Manicures are not inherently gendered, except for you. You are medium length coffin-shaped, French ombre tips decorated by seven jade gems. Your lacquer is imbued with an identity-concealing enchantment. In the Red Blossom Nail Salon, an ancient dragon sets you in the hands of Jess, an employee who needs to be seen as a woman during their cousin's wedding. You are a concession.

The dragon, Linda, also uses your seven jade gems to foretell fated love.

Jess hasn't stopped talking about *her*, Vanessa, since returning to the salon from the wedding. The air smells of varnish. "I need to keep the nails. We're doing dinner tomorrow."

"She doesn't know?" Linda wears her mane in flowing locks. In her human shape, her left hand wears six semiprecious stones inlaid into a fishscale shine. Her right hand has short, natural nails. You are glued-on plastic. Linda dares to express truth.

"She doesn't know *yet*," Jess says, "Not for the first date. If it goes well, then…"

As you leave, Linda picks up a call from her co-owner. She speaks in a dialect too ancient to know, with tones too tender for business.

You are designed to last for weeks. That night's dinner date is easy, even as Jess struggles with you to rifle through their wallet for cash. This noodle spot in the basement food court of a mall is the best in town, a secret they share with Vanessa that is not you. Vanessa's lips are a gradient red. Jess goes in for a kiss, careful you don't scrape her BB cream.

Jess traces their lips with a tip of you hours after. They text Linda, asking if she would replace you when your glue wears out. She demands to know what Jess is scared of. Vanessa is not a disapproving parent nor a dismissive ex. Jess starts to pack solvent.

Jess struggles with soda tabs. You make their duties as a receptionist harder in every way imaginable. They go on two more dates and fall deeper in love. The solvent goes unused for another two weeks.

At the beginning of your third week, you enter Vanessa's bedroom in an apartment shared with two others conveniently out. She showers first. Jess sits on the bed and stares at you. You are an obstacle to their plans for her.

They dig into their bag with shaking hands. You

are easy to remove once your glue is dissolved. They take your thumbs first, inlaid with three gemstones. The four remaining kills the spell.

Vanessa steps out of the shower. "Jessica?" She stops when she sees their face.

Your magic no longer hides the pain of hearing that name. "It's Jess. I'm sorry. Please." Their voice breaks on the last word.

The bed dips. Vanessa places her hands on what remains of you. She is silent for some time. Jess is at their most vulnerable, and you have nothing left.

Then she smiles. "Jess is nice. Did I come off like… We don't have to—"

"No! No. I want to. Here, I feel like I can."

Together, Jess and Vanessa dismantle you.

About the Author

Lark Morgan Lu lives with a collection of succulents and tea. They have been previously published in *Augur Magazine*. Find them at LarkMorganLu.com or on Twitter as @LarkMorganLu.

And Again, We Try

By Allison King

(Third place from 2022 Micro-Fiction Contest)

They call it a cleaning of the tiles, when the mahjong blocks slap against one another. Our hands meet at the center of the table as we clean, sometimes in a warm brush, other times in the sharp jab of a nail. Mother and I have come back to visit her parents on Earth. They are loners in their neighborhood, the last of a dwindling immigrant community. We visit infrequently enough that now we only know how to talk over a mahjong table, through the counterclockwise turns of the game.

"How is the food up there?" grandmother asks me, tossing a tile to the middle.

"Great," I say but she wrinkles her nose. I have missed an opportunity to compliment her cooking.

"You're depriving the boy of his nutrients, living in a pod like that." Grandfather eats my tile into his hand. He is talking to my mother, but speaks only to his tiles.

"But he's also getting the very best education in space exploration." It is a practiced answer. Mother draws a tile.

Grandfather is able to match her tile so it is his turn again.

"But what about his home education? His culture? His family?"

Grandmother matches, mother's turn skipped.

"It's too risky out there," grandmother agrees. Her voice is sweet, placating. "No need to be some sort of space pioneer. Just stay home."

"All the top engineers are looking for kids like me who are used to space," I say, repeating the words of a career counselor.

"Forget careers," grandfather spits. "Is that as important as family?"

"But what about you?" mother counters. It is finally her turn again. She rearranges her hand in small rapid *clicks*, forcing the tiles in line. "What about when you uprooted us? When you brought us to the other side of the world, to a new country? Did you fear I was growing up without traditions? No, and you were right not to. I did things I could never have done otherwise. I am only doing what you once did because it is all I know, and because I am grateful for it."

For an unusually long time, grandfather contemplates the tile mother has thrown out.

"And what if I told you," grandfather says, bringing mother's tile into his hand, "that I regret it?"

He flips his tiles flat on the table, revealing his completed hand. The round is over.

The table is silent. But soon we push all the tiles back to the center, hands brushing hands, slapping the tiles clean. Going through the same motions, we begin another round.

About the Author

Allison King is an Asian American writer and software engineer based in Cambridge, Massachusetts. Her work has appeared or is forthcoming in *Fantasy Magazine*, *Diabolical Plots*, and Paula Guran's *Year's Best Fantasy*. She can be found at allisonjking.com or on Twitter @allisonjking.

Skin Anomalies

By Wen Wen Yang

(Second place from 2022 Micro-Fiction Contest)

When the mark first appeared on my hip, it surprised me the way new moles and old bruises do. Was this self-generating or self-inflicted?

The brown mark was a sharp-edged indentation, long as a pain pill.

I smeared lotion like a ransom.

I pressed scents into my skin that reminded me of my high school friends' mothers. The mothers who had warned us to stay away from boys, but had not warned their sons to stay away from us.

I ignored the mark through the summer. It was a curiosity, not my body's betrayal.

#

Other blemishes appeared down my hip, five in total. They stood out like short black piano keys above the paler stretch marks.

I wondered if my body was keeping score.

What was it counting?

The five spots sometimes dimpled, sometimes bulged, shifting underneath. The discoloration on my hip lengthened and merged at one end.

It looks like a comet with five tails.

Something is surfacing.

#

I accidentally run a thumbnail against my hip. Pain sears up my side. The longest blemish had erupted into a skin tag at some point in the night.

I twist my hip toward the bathroom lights and the skin tag seems to turn. Below it, the other tags have erupted. It looks like fingers.

The end of the longest skin tag shimmers. I tap it, expecting a bead of moisture, the beginning of blood. Instead, it is hard like a nail.

I pinch the largest skin tag.

It hooks around my thumb. It squeezes back.

I pull, digging my thumbnail into its base. I anticipate pain like popping a zit.

Instead, a hand emerges.

I stare at the tiny hand protruding from my hip.

I must remove the parasite from my body. I pull. The sound of suction squelches in my bathroom. I smell metal and rotten fruits. My hip joints rock in their sockets.

The hand emerges, attached to an arm.

My thigh muscle quivers. The arm lengthens to the shoulder. My skin stretches. I twist the arm, attempting to wrench it free.

"Get off me," I hiss.

I grab the manicure scissors from the counter and press the blade against the base of the arm.

The blade slips and bites into my flesh instead. My skin splits open. My blood stains the shoulder as it separates from my flesh.

A head erupts. Black hair is matted to the crown. The eyes are closed. The mouth is open, but not making a sound. I release the arm and the rest of the creature spills out from my thigh. A slimy, tiny baby lies facedown on my bathroom floor.

Is it dead?

How do I get rid of it? Could I shove it back?

No. No.

I will be a devourer of children.

©2022 Wen Wen Yang

About the Author

Wen Wen Yang is a first generation Chinese American, raised in the Bronx, New York. She graduated from Barnard College, Columbia University with a degree in English, Creative Writing. You can find her fiction in *Fantasy Magazine*, *The Arcanist*, *Factor Four Magazine* and forthcoming in *Zooscape* and the anthology "Fit for

the Gods." She tweets @muteddragon and updates
WenWenWrites.com.

Thirteen Simple Steps for Releasing an Old God

By Jessica Luke Garcia

(First place from 2022 Micro-Fiction Contest)

Step one. It happened in a dream. I was naked, pregnant, descending the stairs to the basement of my mother's house, like a Duchamp. I counted the stairs, like Mom taught me when I was a little girl. My breasts ached the whole way down.

Step two. It looked like my landlady's cat, Tofu, from before Nasha and I got married. He was crumpled on the lower landing, a pathetic coffee-cream puddle of broken Siamese. I scooped him up, careful-like, and carried him like a baby. I was halfway up the stairs before I noticed his paws were all wrong.

Step three. His back paws, chicken's claws. His front, human. The sight of those ugly, fleshy man-feet attached to that poor, mewling cat was almost funny afterward. In the moment, my heart dropped.

Step four. I startled awake with an old warning from my mother, half-forgotten, on my mind: *if it gets out of the basement, it gets out of the dream.*

Step five. Weeks later, I found blood in my underwear. Too much. I freaked. Nasha had to remind me we'd gotten drunk with Pai. Gotten creative with a turkey baster, as a joke.

Step six. I didn't put it together then. No reason to. I forgot I'd had the dream at all. After the miscarriage, Nasha and I decided to try for serious. Mars and Declan were keen. The plan was co-parenting, commune-style. Cute.

Step seven. When I had the dream again, the cat was a local dumpster-stray, a skinny tortie. Nasha always liked feeding her brie.

Step eight. I nearly hit the upper landing before I remembered, the cat wasn't a cat at all.

Step nine. It spoke to me then: *you can let me out, or let me in. Choose, or the baby will die.*

Step ten. The cat lied. Our baby had fat rolls like a shar-pei puppy and the biggest, brownest eyes. We were happy together, all five of us. We were happy for two whole years.

Step eleven. Declan and Mars left after it happened. The babysitter's still in therapy. Nasha and I moved apartments, to one without a bathtub. We mourned. We started IUI.

Step twelve. *Your mother chose in. And your grandmother, before her.* I miss the step and catch myself on the railing. The black cat's chicken claws sink into my swollen belly. Its man-feet slap against my breasts.

Step thirteen. *I won't hurt her.* It's got Willam Dafoe's voice. Ridiculous. *You don't have to be the one. Ridiculous cat. Ridiculous dream. I half-believe it this time. Half of me can't, or won't.*

Landing. *You can't have her*, I tell it. *This one's mine. I choose out.* I watch to see if it lands on its ridiculous feet when I let it go.

In a way, it does.

I know I've fucked up when it's still there when I wake: a massive leg, gnarled and hoofed, rising up through the broken ceiling into a storm-green sky, unbound, free at last.

About the Author

Jessica Luke García (any pronouns) is a nonbinary queer writer from the rural borderlands of the American midwest. They are a co-founding editor of *Ripe Fiction*, an online flash journal.

Currently, they live in Las Palmas de Gran Canaria, Spain with their husband, Erik, where they ghostwrite steamy romance novels and court the affections of stray cats. They can be found on Twitter and Instagram @10itemsorjess.

What's up with previous ITAL authors?

We're eternally grateful to our authors from previous volumes for sharing their work with us. As a small thank you, we asked them what they'd like to share about what's going with their writing/lives these days, and this is what they said!

Russell Hemmel

Volume 1 story: *Titawan Delta's Last Message*
Russell has a novella out with Luna Press Publishing, *The Chancels of Mainz* (see our review in the reviews section below). Buy it here: https://www.lunapresspublishing.com/product-page/the-chancels-of-mainz

P.A. Cornell

Volume 2 story: *Nine Lives*

P.A. Cornell is a Chilean-Canadian writer who

penned her first speculative-fiction story as a third-grade assignment (a sci-fi piece about shape-shifting aliens). While her early publications were in non-fiction, she has been steadily selling short fiction since 2016. A member of SFWA and 2002 graduate of the Odyssey Writing Workshop, her stories have appeared in several professional anthologies and genre magazines. Her debut novella, *Lost Cargo*, was published in September 2022. A complete bibliography and social media links can be found at pacornell.com.

RECENT PUBLICATIONS:
Lost Cargo novella (Mocha Memoirs Press) – see our review below!
Lost Cargo - Kindle edition by Cornell, P. A.. Literature & Fiction Kindle eBooks @ Amazon.com.

"In the Grip of Yesterday" and "A Fall Backward Through the Hourglass" (both in Cossmass Infinities)
Cossmass Infinities | Issue 9 - July 2022
Cossmass Infinities | Issue 8 - April 2022

FORTHCOMING PUBLICATIONS:
"Decorative" (To be published in Flame Tree Press' *Compelling Science Fiction Short Stories* anthology, October 2022)
"The Body Remembers" (To be published in DarkMatter's *Monstrous Futures* anthology, April 2023)
"The Smell of Sawdust" (To be published in *ZNB*

Presents in 2023 or 2024)

Maria Dong

Volume 1 story: *A Brief History of KFSD: A Presentation Only Partially Slept Through*
Maria has a book coming out! **Liar, Dreamer, Thief** (Grand Central/Hachette, Jan 10, 2021)
PREORDER NOW: https://www.hachettebookgroup.com/titles/maria-dong/liar-dreamer-thief/9781538723562/

Website: https://www.mariadong.com/link-tree/
TikTok: @mariadongwrites
Twitter: @MariaDongWrites
Instagram: @maria_dong_writes

Ann LeBlanc

Volume 1 story: *Five Tips for Sealing Away an Ancient Evil*
Ann had a story come out recently in Apparition Lit: https://apparitionlit.com/infinite-clay-tablet-memories-sung-into-the-flesh-of-the-world/
Ann has a story coming out in Clarkesworld (!!!) on November 1st. "The Transfiguration of the Gardener Irene by the Dead Planet Hipea" about a sentient fungus having major feelings while eating their gardener.
More to come in 2023—stay tuned! https://annleblanc.com

Marissa Lingen

Volume 1 story: *We Care*
In September, Marissa Lingen had stories in *Asimov's*, *Analog*, and *Daily* SF, with a poem in *Uncanny*. You can keep up with her work at tinyletter.com/MarissaLingen

Aimee Ogden

Volume 1 story: *It Is a Beautiful Day on the Internet, and You Are a Horrible Bot*
Volume 2 story: *A Beginner's Guide to Jailbreaking Your myToast3000™*

Aimee Ogden's short story "A Flower Cannot Love the Hand" from the June 2022 issue of *Beneath Ceaseless Skies* was one of this year's Eugie Award finalists. You can also check out TranslunarTravelersLounge.com to see the latest issue that she and co-editor extraordinaire Bennett North (a Volume 3 author!) have been working on.

To keep up with her, follow on Twitter or check out her website https://aimeeogdenwrites.wordpress.com/

John Wiswell

Volume 1 story: *The Snow White Institute*

Recent stories from John:
"D.I.Y." at Tordotcom follows a disabled boy who couldn't get into wizarding school because of all his medical debt--and now he's got a

plan to change access to magic forever. https://
www.tor.com/2022/08/24/d-i-y-john-wiswell/

"The Coward Who Stole God's Name" at
Uncanny Magazine explores the dark secret
of the world's most beloved man. https://
www.uncannymagazine.com/article/the-coward-
who-stole-gods-name/

"Demonic Invasion or Placebo Effect?" at Sunday
Morning Transport is about demonic scientists
trying to prove they aren't products of
the human imagination--no matter how many
experiments on humans it takes to prove
it. https://www.sundaymorningtransport.com/p/
demonic-invasion-or-placebo-effect

Check him out on Twitter, follow him on Patreon, or
visit his website: http://johnwiswell.blogspot.com

ITAL Author Book Reviews

As a special thanks to Volume 1 and 2 authors with books that have come out since Volume 1's publication, we thought we would purchase, read, and review their work. And wow, were they great! Check out the reviews below.

Russell Hemmel – The Chancels of Mainz

The Chancels of Mainz has the feelings of an erotic gothic historic fantasy horror novella (if such a thing exists, and if it didn't, it does because of Russell Hemmel). The story is well told, following 16th century Germany Inquisitor Hermann De Vylt in his quest to root out witchcraft from the Church, though things do not go as planned...

The novella is a page turner with its excellent pacing and will maintain your interest until the last. I won't spoil the ending, but it leaves much open and left me desperately wanting a sequel.

For those interested, do consider these content warnings: discussions of suicide, plague, and what at first seemed to be sexual assault, but was later revealed to be consensual.

Pick it up here:
https://www.lunapresspublishing.com/product-page/the-chancels-of-mainz

P.A. Cornell – Lost Cargo

Lost Cargo has the vibes of Jurassic Park in space if the main character was a mother who'd lost her child in infancy (this is good, in case you're wondering). It is a heartfelt novella, full of the pains of loss and separation of parents and children, while somehow managing to be a page-turning adventure on an alien planet. The pacing is tight, the characters are memorable, and the emotional wrap-up satisfying. There's lots to love here. Enjoy!

Pick it up here:
Lost Cargo - Kindle edition by Cornell, P. A.. Literature & Fiction Kindle eBooks @ Amazon.com.

Support Us

We hope you loved *If There's Anyone Left* Volume 3 as much as we loved putting it together. Our goal is to make speculative fiction more inclusive, as it should be, as it must be. We're so glad to share these stories with you. All proceeds from this volume will go toward funding Volume 4, so please share with your friends, family, and the world!

-Jason and C.M.

To donate, go to: https://

www.iftheresanyoneleft.com/donate

Manufactured by Amazon.ca
Bolton, ON

30745591R00079